Stark Contrasts

Peter Carroll

Raven Crest Books

ISBN-13: 978-0-9926700-1-6

ISBN-10: 0-99-267001-2

For Sharon and Megan

1. CATS AND DOGS

It all started with the cat. Although, you could argue it started with the dog but, in the end, I don't suppose it matters one way or the other. As the first incident I remember, the tale bears telling.

We lived in a pretty rough housing scheme; the kind of place where you walked into the local pub with a jacket and left with a waistcoat. With burglary rife, lots of families owned a dog you didn't mess with. Our choice of canine protector was a Rottweiler called Bub - short for Beelzebub, which my Dad, who named him, considered quite hilarious. Close up and riled the dog was probably scarier than his namesake.

Bub spent almost all his time outside. Partly due to the small size our house and partly for reasons of security. Our enclosed back garden wasn't overlooked by any neighbours or other buildings, which potentially left the rear of the house vulnerable to attack. However, with Bub in situ, we never found ourselves molested by the junkie housebreakers that so plagued others.

For such a big, scary-looking animal, his temperament, at least as far as our family went, was placid - I can't recall any biting incidents. Unfortunately, this equable disposition did not extend to strangers, therefore he could not be allowed the option of jumping the fence. To avoid any unfortunate accidents befalling passers by, my Dad secured him using a chain tethered to his kennel. This gave him access to the majority of the garden, but left the last few feet just out of reach. Somehow, the cat managed to figure this out.

I'm definitely not a cat person. To be fair, I'm not a huge fan of dogs either, but I really don't care for cats. This particular mangy moggy belonged to some equally mangy neighbours about two houses down from ours. They called it Gordy. By all accounts they were big on Motown and the rumour was a mangy partner called Berry also lived there, but I never saw it near our place. Quite understandably, Gordy spent a lot of time avoiding said neighbours and their foul nest, which helped him become streetwise, tough and sassy. If you could consider a cat a smart ass, then this cat was both smart and ass.

Awake stupidly early one morning, I happened to spend a few moments looking out of my bedroom window, taking in the sunrise, baffled as to why going back to sleep was proving difficult. I never usually found myself troubled by insomnia.

Absentmindedly, I watched Bub pacing up and down, waiting for my Mum to go out and feed him. At the bottom of the garden, on the fence, nonchalantly licking his paw, sat Gordy. The dog appeared agitated but had yet to lose his temper completely. That soon changed.

Gordy dropped from his perch and walked forward a couple of paces. Bub, reacting as if someone had wired his nether regions to the mains, charged headlong towards the interloping feline. Seemingly unperturbed, the cat stood his ground. In fact, the cheeky little bastard sat down. No druggie burglar, no matter how desperate for their fix, would have dared be as bold.

The dog raced to within a matter of inches from the cat, then let out a startled yelp. Running out of chain, he found himself yanked upwards and sideways, before crashing to the ground in a rather undignified heap. He flapped his legs rather comically, trying to regain his footing. Gordy remained impervious and immovable. Once back on his feet, Bub gathered himself: snarling, barking and slobbering in rage, straining at his bonds with every ounce of strength in his muscular frame. Unfortunately for him, even this titanic effort failed to loosen the bolt my Dad used to secure the chain to the kennel, which in turn was dug into the earth for a good couple of feet.

Gordy regarded this display with disdain, hissed like a rattler, and swiped Bub across the muzzle. The claws delivered a comprehensive raking; tiny, retractable, razor blades, drawing thin crimson lines as they sliced through the dog's fleshy face. For such a big dog, the wounds were only superficial. Nonetheless, the blow caused a yelp of pain and surprise, induced a redoubling of effort to swallow the cat in one gulp. I could swear Gordy smirked before taking a second swipe. Evidently satisfied with his morning's work, the cat coolly jumped the fence and disappeared over the other side.

Mum came out to see what all the commotion was about and noticed me looking down from my window.

"What the hell's gotten into the dog?"

I shrugged and turned a circle with my finger next to my temple.

She fetched Bub's food and peace was restored.

For the next three mornings this continued. Gordy would taunt Bub into attack then administer his rebuke before sloping off. The dog appeared too stupid to fathom he couldn't actually reach the cat. It reminded me of Wily E Coyote and the Roadrunner - I half expected Gordy to shout "Meep! Meep!" each time he climbed back over the fence. This situation puzzled me and fascinated me in equal measure. I grudgingly admired the cat for its balls and its remarkable spatial awareness. At some point, it must have sat on the fence working out just how far the chain would reach and judged the safe distance accordingly. On the other hand, I didn't like how smug it appeared. If the cat had taunted the dog once, revelled in the glory of his superior intellect, and then moved on, I would have admired him more. Even twice would not have bothered me too much. As it was, the continual mocking over multiple mornings seemed to spark something in me. I felt the need to intervene. Not only for the dog's sake, but also for mine.

With hindsight, it may have been an absurd conclusion to reach, but somehow it felt like a sleight on me. I imagined the cat looking up to my room each morning and actually saying to me, "Hey loser, look what I'm doing to your dog. There's nothing he can do about it, and nothing you can do about it!". Well, the cat in the ass-hat was wrong. There was something I could do about it.

The next day, on the way back from school, purchases were completed. Once home, I went out to see the dog and made the adjustments. I was pretty happy with my work but would have to wait until morning to enjoy the fruits of my labour. I slept well.

Wakening to the growling preamble I'd grown accustomed to over the past few days, I took up position at the window, ready to enjoy the show.

As expected, Gordy was stationed atop the fence. Bub prowled, disconcerted, but perhaps a touch warier than on previous occasions. Anxiety gripped me: could it be the stupid mutt had finally worked out the cat held the upper paw and, therefore, ruin my surprise. I needn't have worried.

The moment Gordy dropped to the ground and took up his carefully calculated position a few yards from the fence, Bub went ballistic, hurtling towards the gloating cat for the fifth time that week. Just as on all four prior mornings, the cat sat on his mat, totally unconcerned. At the point where the dog would normally have been pulled up short, nothing happened. Before Gordy could react, he found himself impaled on Bub's colossal canines, being shaken about like a bean bag. The dog could hardly contain his glee, or his viciousness, at finally getting hold of his tormentor.

I'm reminded in the telling of this tale about a t-shirt from my student days. The design featured the Coyote holding the Roadrunner by the throat while administering a thorough rodgering with an outsized penis. The caption read, "Meep, Meep now you bastard!"

The cat was dead within seconds. Once Bub realised this, he dropped the lifeless corpse to the ground, and strode off back to his kennel where he sat panting; emanating pride in a job well done.

My own self-satisfaction may have outstripped the levels previously shown by the cat. Sauntering downstairs, out into the back garden and over to the giant guard dog, I felt good about righting a wrong, defeating a bully, allowing Bub to restore his pride. At least, that's what I told myself.

I removed the length of rubber tubing inserted the previous evening and re-attached the chain to the collar as before. The last job was to take a spade and bury the cat at the end of the garden, beside the compost heap. All of this accomplished in time for Mum coming out to feed Bub.

"What are you doing out here at this time of the morning?"

"Came out to see what was bothering the dog."

"And?"

"Oh, I think it might have been a cat. It ran off though."

"Stupid dog! Right, come inside and I'll make you some breakfast."

"Ok, Mum."

A few days later the mangy neighbours called. Turned out they did give a shit about the cat after all. Oh well, that would teach them to look after the next one more carefully. I, of course, pleaded ignorance, gushed with false concern, promised to let them know if I saw the cat around anywhere. I even helped put up some posters on telegraph poles and lamp posts around the area. Somehow, this subterfuge seemed to increase my enjoyment of the whole episode.

Yes, now that I've thought about it, it definitely started with the cat.

2. SOMETHING TO CHEW OVER

It drives me mad: partly the laziness, but mostly the attitude that once it's left their mouth, it becomes someone else's dirty little problem.

I hate chewing gum at the best of times. Pavements are now thoroughly spattered with the stuff - ugly, immovable, embedded in the tar. Sometimes, it looks as if the pavement's developed some form of allergic reaction, breaking out in grey-white hives. Gobbing the stuff onto a pavement is bad enough but, when gum is spat into a urinal in the gents toilet, it becomes a personal bête noir.

The toilet was in a shopping centre near my workplace - the kind of behemoth of commerce that could be found dotted at intervals across London and countless other British cities. A cultural present from our American cousins, which I for one, would gladly exchange for something more suitable or get my money back. Oversized, soulless, anodyne, identikit, crowded and convenient. I deliberately chose the quieter of the facilities, situated at the far end of the centre. With a standard collection of lavatorial furniture and accoutrements; nothing remarkable about it. Until this particular afternoon that is.

If forced to guess, I'd have put his age at about eighteen; wearing a hoodie and an attitude problem. Both of them cloaks, designed to disguise and, at the same time, mark him out as a very particular kind of guy. Jeans hung off his anorexic arse revealing expensive, designer underwear. Knuckles almost scraped the floor. Shambling up to the urinal alongside me, he started to piss. With entirely predictable, casual contempt, he discharged a lump of indigestible chicle into the bowl in front of him, dousing and chasing it around the upturned colander which prevented it from being flushed into the drain. If he'd been listening, the snap, as he placed his straw on my camel's back, would have been plainly audible. However, he couldn't hear it on account of some ghastly form of dance music pulsing through and out of his earphones. One boy, so many irritants.

So, you've just gobbed your gum into the toilet you little dick (literally). Who the fuck is going to fish it out and put it in the bin? You? No? *Really*? You do surprise me. Oh, of course, you're leaving that delightful task to the poor, minimum-wage slave, unfortunate enough to be on duty today. After all, that's what people like that get paid for, right? I mean, if you didn't give them something to justify them being there, they'd be out of a job, right?

Wrong!

I watched the hooded troglodyte head for the sinks, rather improbably demonstrating a regard for his personal hygiene. Unluckily for him, this gave me the time I needed to intercept him at the door as he tried to leave; stick a wedge under it to stop anyone walking in on us. I'd been carrying this around for a while, waiting for the right moment to use it.

I should probably mention at this point that I'm a big guy - as in huge - and this little shit was no match for me. Still, the gun helped persuade him to comply with my wishes, return to the scene of his crime. He wasn't to know it was an unloaded replica.

I indicated he should switch off his music player and hand it over. When he did so, I dropped it into the nearest toilet bowl. His eyes boiled with fury and frustration.

8

"What the fuck, man? That cost me a lot of dough!"

I shook my head, ignoring his protestations. Maybe I was doing him a disservice, but it seemed doubtful he acquired the iPod through entirely legitimate means. The over-the-mirror lights providing illumination seemed to flicker slightly, in time with my anger.

"All right, arsehole. Pick up the gum."

He looked at me, as perplexed as he was fearful.

"Pick it up!"

After a moment's hesitation, he assented, shaking it and holding it with the contempt he deserved.

"Ok, now back in your mouth it goes."

He was aghast.

"Aw, no way! Come on, man. I've pissed on it! What the fuck is your problem?"

"My problem, fuckwad, is arrogant, ignorant pricks like you who think they can act how they please and treat everyone else like shit. Who the fuck did you think was going to go get that gum from the bowl?"

"I don't know, man. The attendant? It's their job to clean the fucking toilets, innit?"

I needed to rein in my temper. The satisfaction in this moment wouldn't come from decorating the wall with pea brain soup, and I didn't need the heat an assault charge would bring. I leant in close, whispered.

"Not today, dickhead. Today, you're going to find out about good manners and consideration for your fellow man or woman. Today, you're going to clean up your own mess."

I pulled back again.

"Now chew!"

He tried to delay the inevitable. Firstly, through aggression.

"Fuck you, motherfucker! I ain't chewing no piss-covered gum!"

As the gun went to his temple, he tried reason.

"Come on, man, you've made your point. I'll put it in

9

the bin. You don't need to make me eat it."

I fixed him in a stare and shook my head.

"Mouth. Now!"

He popped the gum in his mouth, gagging and snorting, only managing a couple of chews before spitting it out on the floor and dropping to his knees, wailing and sobbing.

"Pick it up and keep chewing, you worthless little bastard!"

Looking up, his tear-filled eyes pleaded with me to stop tormenting him. I was unmoved. He reached out mournfully and picked up the gum again, putting it in his mouth on the third attempt. Once again, snorting, coughing and gagging ensued.

"Now swallow."

"What?!"

"Swallow it!"

Defiance made a very brief reappearance.

"Fuck you! I chewed it like you said. I am NOT fucking swallowing it!"

I pressed gun barrel to head, cocked the hammer, at the same time grabbing him under his chin with my free hand.

"You *will* swallow it or I will blow your fucking head off."

He swallowed, sagged to the floor, adopted the foetal position and whimpered pathetically.

The gun went back in its holster. Covering it with my jacket, I stood up, walked across the tiled floor and pulled the wedge from under the door. Almost instantly, a guy came in, stopping when he noticed the hooded baby crying on the floor.

"Is he alright?"

"Yeah, I think he might be a junkie. I offered to help, but sometimes, there's no getting through to his type."

The guy looked at me, then back at the boy and shook his head.

"You're right there, mate. Think I'll use the toilet at the

other end of the centre."

"Yeah, me too."

3. NIGHT-TIME

The deep pulse of the night is pounding in my temples. I pull the darkness in close to me and let it hold me tight. It feels warm and welcoming. It delivers my power. I am at once seen and unseen.

He is near now. I can sense the dread in his veins. The feeling he's trying so hard to suppress. Most of you would not recognise the tells but I can. It circulates with his blood and I can hear him fighting it. It's in his breath, his footsteps, his glance, his shoulders. You would see a confident young man. I see a charade...a victim.

I have selected all of them carefully. They have done wrong - I've seen that. They taunt us, daring us to do something about it; hiding behind rights and excuses. Deny responsibility, blame deflected and renounced. They require chastening and I shall provide. A start was made but I need to finish things off. Complete the circle. Cleanse us of the stain created.

He's wearing the hooded top, shuffling, almost hobbling along in the obligatory manner required of his tribe. The park is deserted, it's late. Any witnesses will likely have four legs and a tail, demonstrate a remarkably similar gait to my boy. In any case, I'm always careful about who sees me. I move with grace and whispers.

I am a shadow, a ghost...a reaper.

He's chewing.

I'm waiting.

He thinks he hears a sound. He does, but without recognition of significance...too late. I am around him, upon him.

No-one sees me. Not even him.

The room is prepared. He cannot struggle now - the anaesthetic has seen to that. It takes me a while to complete all I want to do. Some of it has grace but a certain amount of brutality cannot be avoided. Should not be avoided.

It's a hard lesson learned but he'll be a poster boy for change. An example to take heed of. A warning of what might befall the transgressors. He'll thank me one day for showing him the error of his ways...you all will.

4. STARK

Detective Inspector Adam Stark walked slowly along the hospital corridor, mind not fully on the job in hand, even if it did sound both bizarre and intriguing. To be fair, he was intrigued, but Sarah remained foremost in his pondering.

Sometimes, life as a cop could be shitty. The job, ironically, took no prisoners. You were in up to your neck or you were out - no compromise, no middle ground. Once you made detective grade, it *was* your life. Sarah: more patient than any of the others, more understanding, more forgiving. But even she had a line - a line he crossed once too often.

Still, you make choices in life. No-one coerced him into being a cop, never mind a detective. If a relationship, normality and all that jazz really topped his list of desires, then he could surely have it. It would probably mean leaving the service, but he could make that choice if he wanted to. The unavoidable truth dawned on him as he mulled. Even though Sarah leaving troubled him, it wouldn't make him choose her. They both knew this to be the incontrovertible truth. He was a cop - welcome to his only choice.

"Hello, Detective Inspector Stark!"

The voice hauled him away from his meditation, back into the harsh fluorescent and cloying antiseptic of the hospital.

"Hey, John. How goes it, wee man?"

John Constance was an orderly and a regular contact. He revelled in feeding Stark snippets of information gleaned from patients, and highlighting any admissions he thought might pique Stark's interest. Constance meant well; a cheery, amiable sort, perhaps not the sharpest knife in the drawer but harmless enough.

"I'm good, Detective Inspector, just fine an' dandy. Unlike that poor bastard you're going in to see! That is one weird situation right there."

Eyes twinkling, and yet, Stark sensed an effort being made to suppress disquiet. A false bravado. After many years working in hospitals it was likely Constance had encountered all manner of gruesome sights. Whatever this one involved, it managed to shake a seasoned veteran of trauma. Stark smiled; his own bravado perhaps. Without consciously thinking about it, he held his breath, turned the handle and entered the room.

A young black man lay in the bed, attached to a drip, with his face heavily bandaged. Detective Constable Katz looked toward Stark as he closed the door and nodded the slightest of acknowledgements. Lara Katz was a strikingly attractive young woman. Long, raven-black hair - today tied up tight on the back of her head - a slim, athletic figure and piercing, green eyes. Assigned as Stark's partner about two weeks ago, he was finding it hard to avoid being attracted to her. He got the distinct impression she found keeping things on a strictly professional level with him far less taxing.

"What've we got then, Katz?"

"Dwayne Clements, sir. Aged nineteen, found lying in the street at about three o'clock this morning and brought in here for emergency treatment. Some sick bastard pulled out all his teeth, then sewed up his mouth."

Stark cocked his head slightly and frowned.

"Jeezo. That's pretty severe. Any indication of motive?"

"Oh, the motive is totally clear, sir. The animal who did

it appears to be on some sort of vigilante crusade. He left a note explaining his actions and why we should be thanking him."

Katz reached down, lightly touched Clements on the wrist, picked up an evidence bag from the bedside table with a note in it, and handed it to Stark.

The note was typed on plain, white paper. No words cut from a newspaper, no sloping handwriting in green ink and, no doubt, once forensics completed their once over, would be entirely clean. The message was clear...but also odd. A tirade out of proportion.

To whom it may concern,

For too long we citizens have put up with the erosion of decency, manners, consideration and all the other things that make living together on this small island more bearable. People like Dwayne here think they can do as they please without consequence. Well, I am here to let Dwayne and his like know that there are consequences - I am their consequence.

As he seems so fond of gum, I thought I'd leave him with his - a reminder that respect and consideration for others is something we all need to get our teeth into. If he won't tell you what happened, ask him to spit it out. He usually has no problem with that.

You may may be feeling sorry for him. Don't! He is a warning, a totem. One day he will thank me for this and so will everyone else.

Yours,

A concerned citizen taking action

Taped to the bottom of the note was a stick of chewing gum

"Wait a minute. Is he saying he pulled out all this boy's teeth because he liked gum? What the fuck, and what's with the cryptic comments about respect and spitting something out?"

"I know, sounds like someone who's seriously disturbed to me, sir. Dwayne's still under sedation, so I've not been able to talk to him yet. Apparently, his teeth were yanked out pretty forcefully and with little finesse, but the doc said the sewing was very neat - possibly professional. He was unconscious when he was found, so he's none the wiser either," Katz replied with a certain amount of weariness.

"Has he had any visitors?" Stark asked.

"Not while I've been here, but the next visiting time is at six, so maybe a relative will appear then. Do you want me to hang about and wait for them, sir?"

"Aye, that sounds like a plan. I'll head over to his house and see if anyone's in. I might be able to find out if he had any enemies. You never know, this might be some sort of twisted gang thing. I don't think so, but in this city, you never rule out anything these days."

Katz nodded in agreement and Stark headed for the corridor.

"I'll call you if he wakes up, sir," Katz shouted as he closed the door to the room.

John Constance must have been hanging around, waiting for him to reappear. He strode towards Stark with purpose.

"Told you it was a weird one!"

His face twitched and his head moved sideways then up; an involuntary tick Stark had become accustomed to. Somehow, this morning, the movements seemed more pronounced than usual.

"Aye, sure is, John. Have you heard anything about the lad or the circumstances?"

Stark kept walking as he asked the question.

"Well, I heard he was a bit of a gang-banger. Always in trouble with the cops. One of the nurses recognised him.

She was none too sympathetic actually. Seemed to think he most likely asked for it."

Constance revelled in this stuff: divulging information, being of service, relaying something important to the case. Of course, it wasn't really of great import. Stark reckoned it amounted to little more than tittle tattle. Whenever the guy switched into this mode, Stark lost interest in humouring him and, sometimes less than subtly, made his excuses.

"Ok, John. Gotta dash. Duty calls. Thanks for that. Keep your ear to the ground for me now won't you?"

Stark flashed a winning smile and increased his pace towards the exit.

Constance stopped before he wandered into the lobby and risked being noticed by someone who'd rather he got on with doing the job they were paying him to do.

"Will do, Detective Inspector Stark. See you later."

5. LEARNING

The laughter swept through the corridor as the pitiful, dripping figure of Frankie Monroe trudged past. The cruellest taunts came from Paddy Kerr and his partner in all things unpleasant, Dan Farrell. I didn't laugh. I watched and I thought about Bub and Gordy, about all that was wrong with this situation.

Kerr and Farrell made it their business to humiliate and degrade Frankie Monroe any time they could. Frankie was small, geeky, clever. He struggled with sport and had the misfortune of a late developing body. For a couple of insecure morons, he presented an unmissable target. That day's ignominy came from having his head flushed down the toilet. A tried and tested, old favourite of school bullies the world over.

I wanted to help, to intervene, but I needed to have more about me. Kerr and Farrell may have been insecure, moronic bullies, but they were also two big, strong lads and they would have happily and easily put me in my place physically. I would change that.

It wasn't exactly an inspiration, but it was while watching the Karate Kid one day that it came to me. That's what I would do to gain an advantage, to help poor, downtrodden little Frankie Monroe and his ilk. Martial Arts.

I was a quick learner. A natural. The athletic flow of my limbs combined with an unrivalled work ethic saw me advance up the belts much quicker than most. I knew beyond any doubt when I was ready. The colour of the belt, the exam passed, irrelevant to my true nature, my true ability.

The day it all changed forever, the day I knew why I was here, arrived spontaneously. Sure, I'd thought about what I might do, considered options but, on the actual day, it was instinct drove me on. Rage against injustice. A dark voice inside.

Frankie had been steadily declining. An already quiet, timid boy became invisible, neglected and ignored by all. A pariah. This was before schools took bullying seriously. To most, it was a rite of passage, an unfortunate affliction the unfortunate needed to endure temporarily. It would toughen them up, it wouldn't do any long-term harm. From the other kid's point of view, they avoided Frankie. They didn't want Kerr and Farrell's high beam to sweep over them by association. As long as they had Frankie to pick on, they'd leave everyone else alone.

It was a scorching day, the sun hammering on the tarmac of the playground. Kerr and Farrell pulled Frankie's trousers and underwear down, pressed his bare flesh against the scorching surface. Frankie squealed like a piglet, but this only encouraged them.

"What's the matter little Wankie Frankie? We thought you'd like a bit of hot cock, you little poof!"

The two lads ended themselves laughing at this. Other kids joined in half-heartedly, some trying to ingratiate themselves with the hard men by congratulating them on their tremendous sense of humour. My indignation burned fiercer than the sun overhead.

Distracted by their convulsions, Kerr and Farrell failed to notice Frankie wriggling away, pulling up his trousers and running off.

When Frankie was cut down from the window frame of the janitor's shed later that evening, I made my mind up to act.

The dark was what I needed, what I've craved ever since. Kerr and Farrell, unrepentant, cocksure, drinking in the local park. Celebrating their victory over a foe who never had a chance against them.

I sneaked round behind them, using trees and bushes for cover. Kerr was on a children's swing; one of those used by toddler's, with a small cage around the seat. Farrell leant on the frame, swigging from a large, plastic bottle of cider.

The darkness provided the element of surprise. It was all I needed. The roundhouse kick sent Farrell sprawling, the bottle of cider spraying its contents in all directions as it hit the ground. I pushed Kerr backwards off the swing, his head thumping off the entirely unsuitable hard standing such swings used to be set in. A crescent of crimson spreading.

I grabbed Kerr by his t-shirt and pulled him in close.

"Little Frankie Monroe says fuck you. If you ever pick on a boy like him again, I'll be back. And, next time, I'll do a lot worse than break your scalp open. Do you understand? Do you get it Kerr you fucking moron?"

Kerr groaned, some kind of expletive, indistinct but defiant. A scuff of shoes alerted me to Farrell's return. Before he could get anything on me, I rolled away, pivoted on my hip, stood, kicked his legs from under him. As he hit the ground, I punched him square in the face. His nose crumpled, blood gushing like a fountain in response. I followed this assault up by stomping on both their groins.

They moaned and wept and started pleading. I ignored them, not confident they were getting my message. I kept beating on them intermittently until eventually I tired and decided to make a tactical retreat.

The attack became the talk of the school. Kerr and Farrell humiliated, the biters bit. Bruises lasted for days, their disgrace permanent.

My power established, the message sent, the lesson learnt.

6. STUPID TRUCKER

The rain fell to earth in huge dollops all day. Massive showers interspersed with monumental downpours. The road slick, gutters running with miniature rivers in spate. Vehicle tyres gave off that familiar whoosh as they cut through the surface water; a soothing sound but also a warning. The voluminous spray made it feel like driving in the clouds; cars transformed into aircraft. Such conditions require extra concentration and should require more caution from all those out and about. *Should.*

"He's an absolute arsehole that guy!"

"He certainly is."

"Someone's going to get killed if he keeps that up."

"Yup. Hopefully, just him, but more likely some poor unsuspecting sod with a couple of kids and a dog in the car."

"You know, it doesn't matter how many times you tell some folks, they just don't seem to want to listen or take notice."

A conversation like this would take place between me and Garry most times we were out on the road together. We often admonished folks who were misbehaving, but for some of them, it seemed no amount of telling off or standard punishment would suffice.

When you travel the same route over and over you get to notice repeat offenders. The guy in the truck was doing it again. A leviathan of a vehicle, travelling right on the speed limit, a matter of inches from the back of a small family car. One dab of the brakes from the car and that truck would be making kid pancakes.

"Maybe we need to teach him a different kind of lesson?"

"You mean like the one we discussed last week?"

"Yeah. I think it's about time we did something a little bit different to the usual."

"Ok, I'm game."

Darkness was important, for obvious reasons. The lorry pulled into the petrol station at about nine-fifteen in the evening. The air uncommonly humid for that hour, the breeze still carrying a warmth with it from earlier in the day. The driver dropped from his cab and headed for the toilets. He probably spent around twenty minutes doing whatever he was doing before returning to fill the truck with fuel and buy a few sundries in the shop. With his requirements met, he climbed back into the cab.

"What the fuck?!"

I put my finger to my lips as I put the gun against his ribs and pointed for him to go ahead and drive off.

After driving for about a mile, I gestured for him to pull off the main road. We stopped in a lay-by on a quiet lane, got out and met Garry on the verge. He'd parked his car in front of the truck.

"Come on, mate! What's this all about? If it's the lorry or the load then just take 'em," said the trucker, genuine fear and trepidation in his voice.

Garry gagged him, tied his hands behind his back and blindfolded him, before pushing him into the boot of the car. I took the truck and we drove to our next pit stop.

The cottage was set back off the road, with a driveway wide enough to allow the truck access. It belonged to a friend of a friend, who once let me stay there.

26

Unbeknownst to him, I copied the key to make coming and going separately more convenient for me and my wife. Possibly illegal and definitely a tad rude but, as it turned out, very convenient for the task in hand. Me and Garry had visited earlier in the day and prepared what we needed. We got straight to work.

First off, we trussed him up like a stuck pig. He struggled for a bit, but it was two against one and we knew what we were doing. Once immobilised, we wrapped him in a dark shroud; leaving only his eyes uncovered. Next, we taped his eyes open. It was important he saw the error of his ways. Lastly, we tied him to the bull-bars on the front of his truck. In the dark, it wouldn't be obvious what was going on to anyone watching. It might look a bit odd, but not too suspicious.

Leaning down, I uttered the only words he would hear either of us say.

"It's time for a little driving lesson."

I climbed into the truck's cab and fired up the engine. Its deep, throaty roar comprehensively drowned out any pitiful noises the guy was trying to make.

Garry got in the car and returned to the main road. I followed close behind. Far too close behind.

We drove for around twenty miles. I would drop back about thirty yards and then accelerate to within an inch or two of Garry's bumper, where I would stay for a few seconds, before retreating and then repeating the exercise all over again. We'd spent time practising this manoeuvre in the preceding week, honing our co-ordination. It was terrifying.

Stopping at another pre-arranged spot, just off the road, we untied the guy from the front of his truck and pulled the tape from his darting, frantic eyes. Garry knocked him out cold with a golf ball wrapped in a cloth bag. A simple but effective cosh that left a confusing fingerprint for forensic teams and usually prevented any messy bleeding. We took back the ropes and shroud and

27

laid him across the seats in his cab to sleep it off.

Back in the car, we took off our masks and wigs. Garry spoke on behalf of both our stomachs.

"I'm so hungry I could eat the bloody steering wheel off this car! Let's go and find a kebab shop."

"Good idea. I'll buy you a beer to celebrate a job well done. I don't think he'll be driving right up the arse of the car in front in future, don't you?"

It was good to share these things with Garry. He always showed a great appreciation for my mini-rebellions against life's irritants. A great guy and a pleasure to work with – solid, dependable, always had my back. What more could a copper ask for in a workmate?

7. NIGHT-TIME

I can sense his unease and it feels good. Darkness enfolds me like a cape, enriches me, my power turned up to ten. He will soon learn a far harder lesson than that already received. His macho bravado, his unwarranted disdain: it will soon vanish.

Air slips quietly in and out of my lungs like gentle waves lapping on a shore. A half-hearted breeze drifts listlessly through the car park. A light stabs on and off irritatingly; a sign of neglect and disinterest. You would be hard pushed to call it rain, but moisture definitely surrounds us.

The earlier incident is there with him. I can sense it from the far side of the car park. It's like a solid ball of consternation sitting in his chest; clutching his breath and squeezing tightly. To him, it probably seemed random, unjustified. To me, it seemed incomplete...almost timid.

This is my purpose, my reason for being. I have known this for some time now. I was put here to right wrongs and teach lessons. Some of these lessons will be harsh, but they are necessary. Without them we will sink further into the mire. Flailing around for solid ground as we accept and accede.

Examples require clarity in order to support my mission. There must be no ambiguity of purpose or required outcome.

He is barely breathing. Like the inhalations and exhalations of a moth. His heartbeat a fluttering of wings.

I am watching.

My flame is burning.

I move with the shadows, an apparition, a phantom.

Silent stealth.

All my preparations are in place and things will run as smoothly as I intended them to. Nothing left to chance. No tolerance for error.

He doesn't hear my approach and later, when it's all over, he doesn't hear my departure.

8. A CONCERNED CITIZEN

"Yep, same sicko as before, sir!" said Katz, shaking her head a fraction as she did so.

Stark surveyed the scene. The sky mercifully retained its moisture within a blanket of cloud. Rain would be a most unwelcome guest at this party. Blue and red lights flashed through the night like someone set up an emergency disco, but without music.

The truck ploughed into the back of the van with significant force - the two vehicles locked together in what turned out to be a deadly embrace.

"The guy strapped to the front of the truck is Ernie Martin. Aged fifty eight, married. He was supposed to be driving the truck but our guy tied him to the front and squashed him up against the van like a bug. In fact, the van is Ernie's too."

Stark looked at Katz with a mixture of desire and discomfort that he found strangely pleasing.

"So, is it the same as before? He's a nobody? No ties to organised crime or any such obvious reason for being turned into the filling in a vehicular sandwich?"

"Nope, as far as we can tell, he's just a working Joe, sir. A couple of tickets for minor offences but that's pretty standard amongst guys who drive for a living."

"Where's the note?"

Katz handed him a plastic evidence bag with a plain piece of paper in it.

To whom it may concern,

Sometimes enough really is enough. Ernie was warned more than once about driving too close to the car in front but he didn't want to listen. He's like so many these days - content to do as he likes, happy to risk the lives of others with his selfishness and boorish attitude.

Well, no more.

Just like Dwayne, he's an example, a warning. He won't be the last.

Yours,
A concerned citizen taking action

"He killed him for tailgating? Holy shit, whoever this guy is, he's a grade-A fruitcake!"

"Yeah, but he's clearly well educated and clever. The note is lucid and grammatically sound. There's been nothing for forensics to work with at either scene. Granted, this one's just underway but we got nothing from Dwayne - no prints, no blood, no fibres...diddly squat!"

This perturbed Stark because Katz was right. Despite the truly disproportionate response to the 'crimes' perpetrated by the two victims so far, the killer showed all the hallmarks of a sociopath. But, what kind of sociopath has a social conscience? The whole thing unsettled him; puzzling, bizarre and exactly the kind of case an ambitious detective longs to solve and add to their CV.

"Did Dwayne say much to you once he came round?"

"No, he refused point blank to speak to me. The doctor's reckon it might be some kind of post-traumatic thing. I'm not so sure. Seemed more like a fuck-you-copper kind of thing to me." Katz looked at her feet and then took Stark's gaze. "Did you get anywhere with his family or friends, sir?"

"Not really. I got the impression his Mum was tired of

him bringing trouble to her door. She looked and sounded exasperated. I got the standard, half-hearted defence about him being misunderstood and she couldn't think why anyone would want to do such a thing to him. No enemies she knew of. I think she was trying to convince herself he hadn't been up to something dodgy, more than she was trying to convince me. His friends were even less cooperative. I tend to agree with you about the the fuck-you-copper thing. In the circles he moves in, you just don't help the cops, no matter what."

One of the forensic team gestured to them to come over to the truck.

"What's up, Carl?" asked Stark.

The investigator squatted down and pointed to the mashed face of the dead man.

"It's just the weirdest thing, DI Stark. I know his head's been crushed pretty badly, but his eyelids have been sliced off. The crash could never have caused that. It looks like the twisted bastard did this so he had no choice but to watch what was going to happen to him!"

***

The pathologist's office was neat and tidy. Sparsely furnished, with unremarkable fitments and plainly decorated. A few certificates hung on the wall indicating various medical qualifications, but Stark didn't see any photos on display. A large yucca plant with dusty, drooping leaves stood in one corner. It was doing a valiant job of oxygenating the stuffy little space it found itself parked in; despite the obvious lack of tlc being received in return.

Whenever Stark visited the Coroner's Office it reminded him of a favourite TV show when he was a kid - Quincy M.E. At one time, he harboured ambitions to follow in the great man's footsteps. However, in the end, a lack of the required academic rigour, combined with the lure of policing, saw him move in a different direction. Bizarrely, he once shook Jack Klugman's hand (all the time with mouth agape), after a chance encounter outside a Glasgow restaurant, when his TV hero was on a private vacation. He still loved watching re-runs of the show.

Doctor Sadie Watkins seemed a little harassed when she came into the office. Stark's smile and proffered handshake were both reciprocated rather tepidly.

"Hello, it's Detective Stark isn't it?" she asked and stated simultaneously.

"Aye, Detective Inspector, actually," he replied, instinctively taking out his warrant card and holding it up.

"Oh, sorry, they don't usually send the senior officers down to see me. You're here about the truck sandwich I presume?"

Already, everyone was referring to the case in this way and ergo it was how they were referring to Ernie Martin. It's a sad fact that working in the kind of environment cops and pathologist's were obliged to endure on a daily basis, led to the dehumanisation of victims and a totally unsentimental attitude to death.

"Yeah. I wondered if you'd done the post mortem and whether you found anything I can use?"

Stark considered Dr Watkins a good looking woman in an unconventional way. A short, choppy haircut leant her an almost pixie-like air. Prematurely grey but making no attempt to hide the fact, sculpted cheekbones and a face untroubled by make up as far as he could tell. But without doubt, her eyes were her most striking feature: diamond blue and fierce. Not tall, but lithe and muscular looking. Some form of fitness regime being followed rather than some radical diet. She was certainly no Jack Klugman.

"I did it this morning but I don't think there's much to tell. You knew about the eyelids thing, right?"

He nodded.

"Very neatly done, probably under anaesthetic, as there

34

are traces of it still in his system, along with some alcohol. Below the legal limit, but only just. Otherwise, lots of broken bones, internal bleeding and so on from the impact. No other injuries that I could ascertain were inflicted before the squashing, but it would be almost impossible to tell if there were."

There was a slight pause and she seemed to momentarily drift off before snapping back to attention.

"Did you get anything from forensics at the scene?" she enquired.

"No, not so far. It seems our guy is very careful. Ah, well. Thanks for the update, Dr Watkins. Please let me know if anything else occurs to you while you're compiling your report."

She looked at him rather curiously.

"So, can you tell me, Detective, is it true that whoever did this, did it out of revenge?"

Stark was taken a little off guard by this. He'd been trying very hard to keep the note quiet for now. How had she known? Something in her delivery gave him the distinct impression her repeated demotion of him was no accidental slip of the tongue. He was not warming to this pixie pathologist - unconventionally good looking or not.

"Sorry, Dr Watkins, what makes you ask?"

She shrugged and flashed a sneering smile. An expression that said 'Look buddy, we both know our respective departments are like sieves as far as information goes, so just spill, ok?'.

"One of the forensic team mentioned a note to me in the passing. Something about taking revenge on the guy for tailgating. I thought it was some kind of wind-up. So, was it?"

Stark couldn't decide whether he should indulge her with an answer or not. It was interesting she'd spoken to someone from forensics, therefore knew what evidence was available, but still asked him first. It was almost as if she was testing him in some way; teasing him even. Still, she had spent the last few hours slicing and dicing the victim, so he could understand her curiosity. He did need to be a little guarded though; you never could tell who might have a penchant for spilling their guts to the media.

"Well, it's true there was a note, and it does seems as though our killer has some issues with certain members of society. The thing is though, Doc. I'd appreciate it if you kept this stuff to yourself for now. You know how these things can spiral out of control."

There was a glimmer of a smile and a shrug.

"Oh well, with one less arsehole on the road, my insurance renewal might come down a bit!"

Ah, the gallows humour of those who spend unhealthy amounts of time with corpses. Stark was as toughened to death as any other cop but rarely encouraged these sort of jokes by laughing at them.

After another apathetic handshake, he closed the door behind himself and headed back toward the car.

***

Stark's television flickered and murmured in the corner of the room, but he had no idea what programmes had been vying for his attention since he'd switched it on. Almost as soon as he sat down on the couch, three hours ago, his mind started wandering.

He'd been in London for five years now. The promotion and the chance to join the Met seemed too good an opportunity to pass up. It came just in time to rescue him from his suffocating guilt; bodily removing him from being around the memories that plagued his days and nights. London held out its hand and offered him possible redemption, a chance to start afresh. The guilt gradually receded to sit within his gut like a smouldering ember. He slowly learnt how to avoid it bursting into flame, but every now and again it would lick upwards and scorch his thoughts.

Born in Alloa, central Scotland, his upbringing was a roller coaster of good and bad. He grew up on a tough estate, known locally as the Bottom End. Like all such places, it faced issues related to drugs, gang violence, poverty and deprivation. However, as with all such places (and contrary to popular, middle-class belief), it wasn't entirely inhabited by antisocial yobs and benefit scroungers. There were plenty of good folks; hard working and morally grounded. They may have been lacking many things but ambition and decency were not among them. His parents were two such people. His mum was a school dinner lady and his dad a factory worker. They never fulfilled their own potential academically, but that only seemed to drive them even harder to want more for their kids.

Alloa was not a place he deliberately ran from but neither was it a place he pined for. Sure, he harboured fond memories of school, and some of the people, but the town itself, not so much. In his formative years, he became embroiled in several incidents involving gangs. He never actually joined one himself, but they could still prove hard to avoid. Indeed, one of his front teeth was transformed from enamel to denture thanks to a particularly nasty beating he received around the time of his fifteenth birthday. Still, giving almost as good as he got during that incident, led to the boys involved turning their spotlight on easier targets afterwards.

Thanks to his parents prompting and support, he did well at school without being one of the top four or five students in his year. But, the inescapable pull of the police force reduced academia's importance. If his hankering to follow in Quincy's footsteps had been stronger, things would've been different. Part of his fascination with becoming a policeman (or a fuckin polis as his Dad's next door neighbour liked to call them) sprang from a desire to help people like his Mum and Dad, or his younger self. To try to make life more bearable for the good folks in bad places and do something about the bad folks making good places bad.

Stark attended Tulliallan police college for his basic training. It sat on the outskirts of the small, provincial town of Clackmannan, which was fiscally and geographically convenient as he could live with his folks and not have to lash out a fortune on rent.

It was apparent right away that he possessed a natural talent for police work. He worked hard, solved plenty of crimes, and did all the right courses. Before he knew it, he was thirty-one and being offered a job in London with the Murder Investigation Team or MIT as it was known. He enjoyed the work but he wasn't so keen on London.

London was big - huge in fact - and several times bigger than Scotland's biggest city of Glasgow, where Stark first made his name. The fume-filled, grubby streets and the oppressive, incessant noise were hard to cope with. Worse still, its size ensured respite from these irritants could only be achieved after enduring a journey of several hours.

Like so many Scots, he disliked how impersonal and unfriendly it could be. He was used to saying hello to strangers for no other reason than they were within earshot. Similarly, his sense of humour regularly misfired and left English colleagues baffled or even affronted on occasion. The Scottish wont for relentless piss-taking of oneself and ones friends was not always taken in the spirit intended.

Without consciously being aware of it happening, he began modulating his accent in order to be understood, which made him the butt of many a joke back home. Some of his pals even took to calling him Sheena: in honour of the singer Sheena Easton, famously bottled off stage in Glasgow after addressing the audience with a transatlantic twang rather than her native Bellshill brogue. He'd actually have preferred a bottling to having one of his pals shout 'Get us a drink Sheena!' while he waited to be served in a

Glasgow bar. No matter how many times they said it, his friends never seemed to find it anything less than hysterical.

Discussions about football, humour, school days and music could be difficult to sustain since these areas of culture and identity were so different in Southern England than they were in Scotland. When you're trying to make friends with new folks, it's the things you have in common that help you forge a bond. So often, there was too little to work with.

After five years, the novelty had definitely worn off. Apart from anything else, he would really like to be able to pop round and see his Ma without having to book a flight or sit on a train for six hours.

Snapping out of his torpor, he noticed how late it was, and decided to hit the hay.

Stark turned out the light and pulled the duvet up to his chin; back to sleeping alone...for now. That wasn't the problem preventing him dropping off though. It was the case. The sadism seemed so at odds with the social conscience being proclaimed. It also amazed him that there were no witnesses. The killer must be so careful, precise...

Stark also worried about the moment the excreta connected with the whirly thing. The moment when the press got hold of it. Up until now, no journalist had made the connection between the mutilation of Dwayne Clements and the murder of Ernie Martin and, as yet, no-one from the department had been tempted to leak it. However, it wouldn't be long before the lure of financial recompense proved too great for some low ranking clerk or beat cop to resist. He couldn't blame them really. Then again, the most likely source of information would be this self-appointed moral crusader. Whoever he was, he'd gone to the trouble of leaving messages intended for mass consumption; the fact they'd hitherto gone unpublicised would be unlikely to meet with his approval. All this effort would be for nought if he didn't get his message out to a much wider audience than a couple of cops and a forensic team.

Stark drifted into sleep and a strange dream about Lara Katz seducing him in a distinctly sadomasochistic fashion. Not his first choice of kink if truth be told but, for Katz, he'd give it a bash - literally.

9. A BAD CALL

I'm no different to the next man in many ways. I enjoy a beer, sports and a posh meal with the wife once in a while. She's my second wife as it happens. The first one left me, taking my son with her, but sometimes these things work out for the best. I get access and our relationship is amicable and cooperative as far as the lad goes. To be fair to number one, I wasn't as faithful as I should've been. It's a behavioural problem I really should've grown out of by now. I don't know what makes me find monogamy so difficult to achieve – even when I'm deeply in love.

The current Mrs and me have a favourite restaurant but it's a bit pricey. Actually, it's frigging extortionate and we can hardly ever afford to go there. When we do, it's for something really special like our anniversary, or a worryingly significant birthday. This time it was due to her promotion at work. She's the brains of the operation. And the beauty.

As restaurants go, it's a fairly big place; set across two floors, with a mix of open tables and more intimate booths. It is at once modern and traditional but extremely nicely done. I suspect it cost a whole heap of cash to get it kitted out. These qualities help it attract the rich and famous, as well as the fiscally challenged, indulging themselves every once in a while. Unfortunately, it has always been my experience that there's a certain type of money that deletes the manners and consideration most of

41

us have in such social situations. On a couple of previous occasions our enjoyment of the night had been diminished by loud-mouths, braying about how they made their fortunes and how they did it all themselves. The worst intrusions into our cherished and infrequent moments of indulgence were perpetrated by the mobile-phone-shouters. Tonight, the guy in the next-door booth was going to learn a very important lesson in restaurant etiquette.

We were not even finished ordering our meal when he started.

"Yeah, that's right, man. I'm down at Cardoza's. Slumming it with the football players and a few wannabes."

Insert unheard reply from fuckwit at other end of the line.

"HAHAHAHA!"

Insert etc.

"No, I tell you what, it's going downhill. They let all sorts in these days."

Insert...

"Waitress is a babe, though. Reckon I might have seen her in a movie...if you know what I mean! HAHAHAHA!"

Insert...

"Ok, no problemo. Catch you later, man. Yeah, nice one! Ciao!"

My wife looked at me and sighed. I shook my head. The waitress blushed. We ordered and settled back to enjoy the food and each other's company. The shouter had other ideas. Versions of the initial conversation rattled out over and over again. Sometimes more profane, sometimes involving some sort of business transaction. All the time, immensely irritating.

After the starter, I made a visit to the bathroom and took stock of his set-up.

I never got a good view of his face because he sat in

the booth with his back to me. His date was a blonde, naturally. Well, I doubt she was a natural blonde, but nonetheless, the nouveau riche clichés kept on coming. Half-eaten food, an ice-bucket with Krug champagne, a blinged-up smart phone lying out on the table for all to envy. Even without seeing him well I could tell he was young - early to mid-twenties maybe - immaculately groomed and dressed in the kind of designer suit I would need to work a couple of lifetimes to afford. Wealth had afforded him a lot of things, but class was not one of them. Here he was, in the company of a beautiful, nubile young lady, with plenty of cash and the vigour of youth on his side, and yet, here he was, ignoring her, shouting his mouth off to numerous unseen callers, and leering over the waitress. He may have professed contempt for footballers, but he was a Premiership arsehole in my book. I made some preparations in the toilet and returned to my main course.

The shouting and profanity continued. A waiter asked him politely to tone it down and he gave him a mouthful of abuse. Doubtless, the restaurant were prepared to tolerate a lot more bad behaviour from a client spending the kind of eye-watering sums he was lashing out. Personally, I think this was a bit of a short-sighted and short-term approach. If this was my place, he would long since have become intimately acquainted with the pavement outside. As we completed our desserts, he got up and headed to the toilet. I made my excuses to my wife and followed suit.

He entered the stall, making the fatal error of failing to lock the door. I walked in straight after him and, before he could turn or react, I smashed him round the temple with the golf ball in a bag. He fell to the floor unconscious. I closed the door, slid the bolt across and got to work.

I donned a pair of surgical gloves and gagged him with his own tie. Then, retrieving the mobile-phone from his pocket, I searched through the menus for his number;

scribbling it down on a small pad. Next, I used a rope to tie him to the cistern, positioning him so his torso was across the pan. I undid his belt and zip, pulled his trousers and boxer shorts down to his knees. Finally, I took out the condom and applied the lube.

Back at the table with my wife, we finished our aperitifs and paid the bill. Outside the restaurant I stopped at a pay-phone.

"I just want to make a couple of calls. You go on ahead to the car. I'll catch you up."

"Why not use your mobile?" asked my wife.

"Oh, the battery's running flat. Anyway, I sometimes get sentimental for the good old days,'" I said, winking at her as I punched in the number.

"Yeah, if only that dickhead at the next booth had felt the same!"

I laughed as the number rang out and I got through to the answer machine. It was the voice of a sultry young woman.

"Leo can't take your call right now as he's too busy being successful. Leave your message and he might get back to you."

Something suddenly struck me about the name. Leo. Why would I know someone like him called Leo? I let it ride but something was nagging.

In the toilet of Cardoza's a couple of waiters were washing their hands when the distinctive, but rather muffled ringtone of one Leo Corantelli struck up.

One of the waiters whispered to the other.

"I would love to shove that mobile up the arrogant bastard's arse!"

"Yeah," replied his companion, "too right, mate."

They chuckled quietly and headed back to the restaurant.

I left my message and hung up.

10. A HOUSE CALL

Ernie Martin's house was just as Stark imagined it might be: a hovel. The estate it sat in was thoroughly depressing and depressed. A congregation and aggregation of the discarded and forgotten, the ill-educated, poorly raised and all manner of other unfortunates. There were a million different hard luck stories within the confines of this place. So many flats and houses ending up as containers full of broken dreams, misery and disconnection: the poverty extending far beyond what cash people had in their wallets. You could add to this mix the parasites and the chancers. The ones who were exploiting the desperate or bucking the system. If you didn't *have* to live in a place like this, you would never choose to. It was like his old home in Alloa but on steroids - whatever problems the Bottom End faced, multiplied a thousand times. His desire to help the good people drowning in such seas of inequity was undiminished but, sometimes, he would feel overwhelmed by the scale of his task when he visited an area like this.

Mildred Martin was a mess. Face ruddy and bloated; like she'd been crying and drinking for a week - and not necessarily in that order. Her shabby clothes, bloodshot eyes and trembling hands, aptly offset by her bird's nest hair. A middle-aged woman whose life had panned out very badly, and she knew it. Once upon a time, Mildred had been a pretty, little girl with hopes and dreams and a future. But now, little more than a cypher; one of the walking dread, shuffling around the estate, alive in strictly biological terms only.

She chuffed feebly on a succession of cigarettes, each allowed to burn to the point of depositing ash on her carpet between puffs. Not that it made much difference to it's dirtiness. The place would probably have made a cockroach nauseous. A glass of neat vodka was topped up periodically throughout their conversation and alternately glugged or sipped as the mood took her.

"He was a good man," she slurred, "and he worked hard and I loved him."

"I'm very sorry for your loss, Mrs Martin, but I need to ask you a few questions about Ernie and what happened to him."

She slurped her vodka again but he hadn't the heart to force her to desist.

"You need to find them two boys what scared the livin shit out of 'im the other week!"

Stark, knocked right out of his stride by this, shot a look at Katz. She seemed equally rattled.

"What do you mean, Mrs Martin?"

"He was taken hostage by two men. They tied him to the front of his truck and played chicken with their car. He was terrified. He told the local bobby but that fat tub o' lard never did nothin about it. I never thought they'd come back and finish him off though."

Her shoulders hunched and she let out a sob, quelling her fragile emotions with a quivering draw on her cigarette and a glass-draining gulp.

"Are you saying that two men did this to him a week before he was killed?"

She wiped snot from her top lip with the sleeve of her blouse and sniffed.

"Yeah, that's right! And I want you to catch them evil bastards and throw away the key for what they done to my Ernie!"

Stark and Katz looked at each other and, without

consciously planning it, raised their eyebrows in unison. It was very rare for vigilantes to work in pairs or teams. You could expect that kind of thing more often when gangs or drugs were involved. Not only that, but the notes left at the scenes so far made no reference to there being multiple people involved.

"Mrs Martin, I need you to tell us all the details you can remember but can you please do me a favour?"

"What's that, son?"

"Can you stop drinking? We need to be sure you can recall this properly and not miss anything out. Every detail you can give us might be crucial in finding whoever did this to your husband."

It was obvious that even stopping now would make little discernible difference to the quality or veracity of her evidence. They needed to leave her to sleep it off and get her into the station for a full, fully sober interview the next day.

Back in the car, Katz was first to break the silence.

"Do you believe her or do you think the old coot is getting muddled up with all that vodka sloshing around in her brain?"

"She seems pretty convinced but I suppose it might be an alcohol-induced false memory." He looked off into the distance, considering.

"Nah, it's just not the kind of thing you would make up or blurt out to a cop unless it was true...surely?"

Katz shrugged. "I guess."

"No, really, I think it's just a wee bit too off the wall to invent unprompted. Anyway, at least it gives us a start. It also means we've got two bad guys now and not one. It would explain the physical advantage over the victims but it also gives me some hope we'll catch them. Partnership is much harder to get right than being a lone wolf."

"Don't I know it, sir!" quipped Katz.

They both laughed. The first glimmer of a thawing

Stark had seen so far. His hopes upped a notch. Why, he had no idea. There was so little to be gained from turning your work partner into your bed partner. Katz was young, beautiful, cool as, and one of the most focused colleagues he'd ever encountered; of either gender. He was just horny. Simple biological urges, which required resistance.

"By the way, did we get anywhere with looking for CCTV footage from the park where Dwayne was attacked?" Stark asked.

"No, sir. The park itself isn't actually covered because it's too dark for any footage to be useful. The council's been saving money on lights apparently. They have dummy cameras and signs up as a deterrent but there's nothing for us to look at."

"Ah, well. Nobody had CCTV in the seventies and the cops still managed to solve crimes, so we'll just need to look for some other way to catch these guys." Stark added wryly.

"I suppose so, sir."

11. MOTION SICKNESS

Every workplace has one. An annoying, officious dick that likes to do everything by the book. Obsessed with what people fail to do, seemingly incapable of ever recognising achievement. Mine had one too.

Morris Hargreaves reached his late fifties still buttoned up about everything - from starched collar to attitudes about sex. Bitter and resentful about life, it was apparent he tried to make himself feel better by making others feel like shit. Incidents resulting in tearful and stressed-out colleagues making for exits and bathrooms abounded.

He cultivated a hard on for me that would've made the 70's porn star John Holmes jealous.

What pissed him off most was his inability to intimidate or stress me out. I found his frequent petulant outbursts pathetic for a man of his years and standing. In fact, on at least two occasions I laughed in his face. Give him his due - he was a persistent little fucker. I could expect at least one dressing down a day and, if I was really lucky, several. It was a battle of wills he would never win.

By a strange quirk of fate, and much to my chagrin, I needed to deal with Morris Hargreaves in another aspect of my life. He was Chairman of the committee that ran my son's swimming team. His granddaughter was a junior champion, he was a prize prick.

Whenever anyone made a suggestion as to how funds could be raised, communications might be improved, uniforms could be sourced more cheaply or anything else minor or major pertaining to club matters, they got the same answer.

"You'll need to table a motion."

Nothing could ever be decided there and then. Nothing could be ad hoc. Everything needed to follow the due process set out in the club constitution. It added unnecessary delay but, crucially, as far as Hargreaves was concerned, everything went through him. This rendered him gatekeeper and backstop for all things swimming club. People such as Hargreaves are drawn to such positions for all the wrong reasons. They delight in exerting power over others and always seem to take life far too seriously.

Given our strained relationship, I avoided volunteering ideas or suggestions unless I was sure he already agreed with them. He waited with baited breath whenever a committee meeting was in session, willing me to contribute something radical, just so he could slap me down. I kept my counsel and he seethed with frustration. It made the meetings more bearable for me.

"Ok, but you'll need to table a motion."

It wasn't a particular incident as far as I can recall. It was more like Chinese-water-torture. A drip, drip, drip into my subconscious. He must have filled the tub and I needed to pull the plug to prevent a flood.

"TABLE"

"A"

"MOTION!"

Accessing buildings covertly didn't usually present a big challenge for me. The swimming club committee met in a back room at the local church hall. Tight security was unnecessary - nothing worth stealing ever spent the night there. As a result, this covert entry proved to be a cakewalk.

The committee meeting was set to begin at eight the next morning. Hargreaves liked to drag things out, so he started early. As a keyholder, he was always punctual. For once, I would be there well ahead of the kick-off to ensure I could enjoy the moment.

At seven-forty-five I found myself outside the church. The club secretary, George Amberry, also waited. He only experienced being bawled out for lateness once, but it was enough to ensure he never ran the risk of getting there *after* Hargreaves again. Not the most assertive of guys, but a very good accountant by all..er..accounts. Conversation between us didn't extend much beyond a 'How are you?' and remarks on the weather. Blue sky, sixty degrees, as it happened.

At seven-fifty Hargreaves rolled up in his twenty year old BMW. Almost all his life took place in some form of suspended animation; a golden age of times gone by. He could easily afford a new car, but he'd rather spend hours maintaining and polishing the one he bought in his prime. He shot me a quizzical look - with just a dash of healthy (and, as it happened, well-placed) suspicion. I nodded in faux deference and politeness.

Hargreaves, carrying a bundle of folders and papers, turned the key in the lock and let the door swing open. He strode forward with his purposeful, military gait. Around half-way down the hall he stopped dead in his tracks, dropping the paperwork to the ground where it slid in various directions across the varnished floorboards. His hand went to his mouth, then he bolted for a waste-paper bin and held it up as he retched and dry-heaved.

George Amberry edged a few yards further into the hall, then stopped.

"Holy shit!"

"Yeah, maybe, but even if JC himself evacuated it, I don't think they'll be handing *that* out at Communion on Sunday, do you?" I quipped.

George spluttered with laughter.

The pile of faeces in front of Morris Hargreaves' nameplate was copious and horribly pungent. A few flies were already in attendance.

I whistled softly and looked over at our chairman, staring back at me ashen-faced and dumbstruck.

"Oh dear, Morris. Looks like somebody tabled a motion - literally!"

12. LEO THE LION

Leo Corantelli was very upset. Very, very upset. What occurred in Cardoza's qualified as the single most humiliating moment of his life. The restaurant staff were intolerably smug when they found him; the paramedics and hospital staff snickered, pointed, talked behind his back. This was not paranoia on his part, this was fact.

The removal of the phone left him sore, and for the first few days afterwards, taking a dump was no laughing matter. But, he wouldn't be leaving it there. Oh no! The distress, discomfort and ignominy was eclipsed by a raging fury. The prick responsible for his unhappiness had made the biggest mistake of his soon-to-end-painfully life.

Leo was the youngest son of Carlo Corantelli, one of the the city's best connected gangland bosses. His father could never have imagined a mobile phone would be pulled from his son's butt, even though he thought the sun shone out of it. What Leo wanted, Leo got...and Leo wanted this guy dead. Luckily, violent notoriety prevented anyone from the hospital or restaurant from contacting the press about his admission. Leo also made sure none of his father's crew knew exactly what happened to him. As far as they were concerned, this would be the usual no-questions-asked revenge for crossing the spoilt son of their boss. Questions were unnecessary; they did as they were told.

The attack had been bad, the reaction of the restaurant

staff and medics angered him, but the message the guy left on Leo's answering service caused his rage to spiral up towards the stratosphere. This guy would be very, very sorry that he ever crossed Leo.

Leo walked into Cardoza's at ten o'clock in the morning with three, large goons in tow. The duty manager, newly arrived, was returning to lock the front door after cancelling the alarm.

"Hey guys, we're not open until midday. Do you want to make a reservation?"

His sunny disposition smacked of someone well-drilled in customer care. Unfortunately, this did not prevent him being punched to the ground.

"How about that for a reservation?" spat Leo. "Do you remember me, you little prick?"

The hapless manager, head spinning, blood dripping, looked up and it dawned on him who he was dealing with.

"Yes, sir, Mr Corantelli, I remember you. You're a very good customer."

The platitude failed to make any dent in the violent intentions of his one-time patron. Leo booted him heftily in the midriff and the young man folded in half, winded and disorientated.

"Damn right I was a very good fucking customer! But you ungrateful shitbuckets let someone attack me on your premises and then laughed at me after it happened!" Leo stood with hands on hips, glowering with seething contempt. "Well, you won't be laughing any more!"

He aimed another kick at the prone manager, then signalled to one of the goons to pick him up.

"Right, get me your reservation book."

The manager led them (if you count being roughly shoved as leading) over to the bar where he pulled out a large, leather bound book.

Leo snatched the oversized diary, flicking through the pages until he found what he needed. Friday the ninth. He tore out the page, letting the rest of the book fall to the floor, and scanned down to table fourteen - a surname, nothing else. Although it hardly seemed possible to boost it any further, this setback increased his displeasure.

"Is this all you've got? Do you slack bastards never take a mobile number or an address from customers who make a booking?"

The now whimpering, trembling manager tried to speak, but it just came out as a sort of whispered squeak. He got a slap round the face for his trouble.

"Speak up you pathetic sonofabitch!"

"I'm sorry, Mr Corantelli. We store the number on the phone in case of a no-show and we can black list them but, if they turn up, we delete it," he managed, shrinking back defensively once he'd finished.

Leo simmered. He'd been sure this would be his way of finding the bastard but, a surname, with nothing else to embellish it, was bordering on useless.

"Do you know this guy? Is he a regular?"

"I don't think so, Mr Corantelli. I've worked here for six months and that's the first booking I remember seeing from him and his wife. He definitely doesn't come here as often as you do."

"Ha! Well you can kiss my arse from now on, pal. Leo Corantelli will no longer be frequenting this shitpile.

"Did you talk to him? Got any information I can use to find him?" barked Leo.

"No, I didn't deal with him personally, sir, other than greet him and show him to his seat."

Leo looked around the restaurant, thinking.

"Do you have security cameras?"

"Yes, sir."

"Where do you keep the tapes?"

The manager's anxiety deepened significantly in advance of the answer to this question. An answer that seemed a dead cert to bring him the next instalment of hostility.

"We don't keep them here, sir. They're backed up electronically and downloaded to our central computer in New York."

Leo looked up at the ceiling, a low snarl turning to a deep growl, then a howl of rage.

"FUCK!"

He grabbed the manager by the lapel, pulled him in close and stuck a business card into his shirt pocket.

"If that fucker comes back here, I want to know right away. Do you understand?"

The young man nodded vigorously. "Yes, sir, I do and I will."

Leo shook him loose and headed for the door. He stopped just short of it and turned around.

"You know I can make things a lot worse for you if you mention a word of this to anyone, don't you?"

The manager nodded.

Leo and his companions swept out of the restaurant and into the crowded street. The manager, Myles Gilmore, slumped to the floor and put his head in his hands, guts churning, nose throbbing, head spinning. A bona fide gangster just threatened him with violence and he'd probably become an accessory of some sort in the murder of one of his customers. He'd definitely experienced better starts to a day at work.

13. WHEN PUSH COMES TO SHOVE

The hives of London were emptying and the airless station swarmed with its usual rush-hour influx of drones. People impersonating sardines, eyes glazed over, desperate to escape the tin. Sweat, anxiety, claustrophobia, bad breath, fractious children and frazzled parents, business men checking watches, and pickpockets sizing up potential victims. A heaving throng of eye contact being avoided and wish-I-was-anywhere-else moroseness.

I hated having to use the Tube. A necessary evil - I always needed to psyche myself up to embark on whatever journey might be required. The way so many people accepted such things every day of their working lives totally confounded me. No salary could ever compensate for enduring this hideousness with any degree of frequency.

Tube stations are always warm but at the height of summer they are something else. You could see folks wilting as they alighted from the escalator. On this particular evening, I could swear the temperature inside was greater than that found in the bowels of Hades. In fact, it seemed entirely plausible to me that once you reached the platform, you really had stumbled into said bowels. There was no doubting it was a crap way to spend my time. Only as a train approached, and air was drawn through the tunnel, did people find relief forthcoming.

My train pulled in, the temporary draught evaporated

and the mad scramble began. Incredibly, I managed to board the carriage nearest me almost straight away. But, as ever, my travails did not end there. It is, I suppose, human nature to want to get out of a bad situation as quickly as possible. However, the irony was, in jamming onto the train itself, people merely recreated the hellish discomfort of the platform they were so desperate to escape.

The guy looked about fifty and really should have known better. In a mind-boggling display of bad manners he barged onto the train with an out-sized suitcase, big enough to pack away a small planet. He shoved a pregnant woman so hard she nearly fell to the ground but he paid her no heed - or that of the protesting onlooker who tried to offer her assistance. As the doors closed, he continued to push and prod anyone unfortunate enough to be in range. Outrage surged though me like an electric shock.

That's the thing. The morale-sapping experience of Tube travel is exacerbated and magnified by the likes of that wanker. Rudeness and selfishness tipping off any scale used to measure it. Well, today, this particular ill-mannered tosser picked the wrong train.

As we hurtled between stations I kept an eye on Rude-boy as I decided to call him. It was too much to expect he was going to the same station as me and, sure enough, he wasn't. I stuck with him though. My wife would understand when I explained the reason for my tardiness; she's a very reasonable woman. My son, unaware of a specified rendezvous time, wouldn't notice.

I edged toward Rude-boy whenever there was a changeover of passengers at a station. After one such stop and the resulting minimal increase in space, he managed to bag a seat: this miracle achieved by barging a frail, elderly gentleman out of the way. His smug expression afterwards suggested pride in doing so. Insult, piled upon injury, piled upon insult. I was going to enjoy sorting Rude-boy out.

Eventually, I got close enough to subtly reach down

and remove his luggage tag. If I lost sight of him in the mob of a crowded station, I would know where to find him later.

The station where he disembarked was less crowded than the one where we both first boarded. The number of passengers on the train had also thinned out - we were no longer melded together as if one homogeneous lump of humanity. I waited for him to step to the platform, then followed closely behind, confident there was little chance he'd become suspicious of me. Grudging tolerance of uncomfortable closeness to strangers was the way he'd just spent the last thirty five minutes. My hunch proved correct and, as we left the platform, he was oblivious to me shadowing him.

At the top of the escalator, sunshine bathed us. It was a different kind of heat up top compared to underground; somehow more bearable and with the welcome relief of fresh air being wafted on a gentle breeze. I could feel my shirt sticking to my back and longed for a refreshing shower.

This was one of those affluent areas of the city less familiar to me. Folks living here - and presumably that included this pushy bastard - were in an income bracket several notches above me. Just like the mobile phone guy, he was proving money alone could not buy you class. Rude-boy stopped to mop his brow and put on some shades. I also popped on my sunglasses: the brightness of the outside dazzling in comparison to the artificial light of the tunnels.

He set off again at a brisk pace. I accelerated and, once within range, tapped his heel, causing him to trip. He sprawled full length, exclaiming loudly as he did so; shades clattering ahead of him on the pavement. I deliberately tumbled on top of him, making sure my elbow dug heavily into his ribs.

"Hey, mate, are you ok?" I asked, in as concerned a voice as I could muster.

As we disentangled ourselves and I offered my hand to help him up, he shouted with vehemence and no small degree of indignation. "What the fuck?! You just tripped me up!"

"Whoa! No way, mate. I was walking behind you and you suddenly slowed down. I couldn't get out of the way and we fell together. If anything, *you* tripped *me* up! I suppose that's what you get for trying to help these days."

Warming to my part as the real victim, I withdrew my hand and folded my arms.

Rude-boy got to his feet rubbing his knee, his trousers torn, blood spreading darkly across the light coloured fabric. He nursed his (hopefully heavily) bruised ribs. Unfortunately, the impact hadn't been sufficient to inflict any serious damage to the prick.

"I'm sorry..." he said in a rather suspicious, unconvinced tone.

A female passerby pretended to take no heed; probably unwilling to get involved in what looked like a heated disagreement between two big blokes.

I stepped back in the full knowledge of what I was about to do. The very expensive eye-wear crunched under the heel of my boot. Oh, that felt good!

"Hey, watch where...oh for fuck's sake! Those cost me a fortune!"

He scrambled to the floor, desperately trying to reassemble them - but I had done my job with a finality that would render repair impossible.

"Shit, sorry about that. I didn't see them there."

"Yeah? Look, just leave me alone will you. If this is your idea of helping people then I'm not impressed!"

The pitiable wanker cradled the shattered shades like a precious child, looking like he might actually start weeping over their passing. I shook my head, trying hard to suppress the laughter straining to burst forth.

"Ok, whatever, mate."

With that, I continued up the street a way before

doubling back toward the station. I left him checking himself over and reaching for a mobile phone to make a call of some kind. The disorientation of a random encounter with a stranger worn like a fluorescent tabard. My satisfaction tempered slightly by the lack of involvement from any paramedics. Never mind, it was a small victory and a necessary release on the valve. A cuff round the ear of bad manners and the blinded insularity of some city dwellers.

As predicted, once united with the family, my wife was very reasonable and my son easily placated with ice cream. I could get on with enjoying one of my weekend's with the boy. Wife number one away doing whatever she did when given this temporary fortnightly freedom.

When I told him about it, Garry thought the whole thing hilarious.

14. NIGHT-TIME

I have been patiently waiting for this opportunity. A character trait that has always stood me in good stead. Patience ensures mistakes are avoided. Persistence ensures jobs get completed regardless of obstacles, inexperience or difficulty. The precise, requisite set of circumstances for this lesson have not been easy to come by. But, here and now, all the essential elements are aligned. Patience and persistence, my comrades and confidantes.

This one's not as apprehensive as the others. He doesn't realise how wrong he is to be so casual. Still jostling, still entirely focussed on number one. Still unaware of the wrong, the danger, the wrath.

My power is uncomfortably low. This flickering ember is alien to me. I'm used to it burning like a thousand suns. I almost feel too weak to see this through. I crave the dark, I need the dark, but it cannot be dark in here. I have no choice, no influence over this. I take solace from the darkness nearby until it's ruptured by headlights. Light is my kryptonite.

I don't like crowds - it's risky. Privacy affords time to tidy and repair, make good any spillage or oversight. An audience might mean a witness but there's no other way to make the point which needs to be made. It has to be here, in the light. It has to be now. Yes, I'm weakened, but far from impotent.

I move slowly; like wading through human treacle.

The heat rises.

The lights burn.

The wind blows dragon's breath.

I am fighting against the light.

I move forward and, this time, the tap on the heels is final.

A surge of bodies, voices, grinding metal screeching in protest, hysteria.

I melt away.

He won't be the only one to get the message this time. I've made sure of that.

15. BLOOD ON THE TRACKS

Stark yawned like a hippo, giving the Bobby an uninterrupted view of his epiglottis. He held up his badge and crossed the tape. It was far too early in the morning to be dealing with this kind of shit. He was not a morning person. Mornings were for the birds and the paper boy, and they were welcome to them. On more than one occasion, he pined for the certainty and solace of constant back shifts. Great for the guy who can't get out of bed unless someone sets fire to it, but not exactly a boon socially. Ah, the job giveth and the job taketh away.

The station hummed with activity. White-suited forensics guys, uniformed cops, a couple of plain-clothes and, unfortunately, a journalist. He recognised Floyd Callahan from The Daily News even from behind. A bean pole of a man - by all accounts six feet seven inches tall - with a shining bald pate. An ex-NBA professional player who retired early due to serious injury and a rumoured fondness for falling down water. Like many guys in his position he started out as a TV pundit, then qualified as a sports journalist, but gradually branched out into other areas over the years. The opposite of that Sting song – a New Yorker in England.

His physicality and accent were not the only things that made him obvious. Floyd Callahan had a penchant for wearing brightly coloured trainers in combination with a designer suit. Stark thought he might have taken the concept of smart/casual a little too far. Callahan insisted it allowed him to sit at a dinner table and look good, but when a story broke, he'd be first there because he could run. A logic...of sorts.

As Stark approached, Callahan swivelled instinctively on his heel, broke out his best Cheshire Cat grin. It was no use, as much as Stark disliked the majority of journalists, he couldn't help but warm to this gangly, eccentric hack. After all, he wasn't a proper journalist - well not in the sense of what most people would consider one to be. Stark reciprocated.

"Hey, Floyd. How the hell did you find out about this?"

The goofy giant's smile stretched to breaking point and he tapped the side of his nose.

"Now, now, Adam, you know a good journalist never reveals his sources!"

"Well, you can tell me then coz *you're* not a good journalist!" quipped Stark in response.

"Touché, Starky, touché! How the devil are you anyway my friend?"

They shook hands warmly, tapping each other on the right elbow with their left hands. A sort of slightly more professional, manly version of a hug.

"Well, I would be a lot better if I was still in my bed instead of dealing with this kind of crap at seven-thirty in the morning!"

Stark scanned around and spotted Katz; squatting down track-side, deep in conversation with one of the forensics guys. She'd beaten him to the punch again. Every crime scene they'd covered recently, she seemed to have the jump on him. It elicited a stab of paranoia. Was she out to show him up? Ridiculous. She merely tried harder than the average trainee to impress him and his superiors. It annoyed Stark but she provoked diaphanous unease in him. Despite working together for a few weeks, she'd told him nothing of her private life and made no enquiries about his. A kind of cold detachment, bordering on aloof. If she wasn't so damned hot, he'd find it easier to dislike her for it.

"Sorry, Floyd, I'll catch up with you in a bit. Need to go and talk to my partner, see what the lie of the land is."

"Ok, Starkmeister. No problem. Once you know some more, you can come and tell me all about it," said Callahan, winking as he did so.

Stark smiled, shook his head, lowered himself off the platform onto the track and made his way over to Katz.

His inscrutable workmate looked over her shoulder as he approached and stood up.

"Hi, sir. Meet Calvin Jacobs: victim number three of our vigilantes."

"What? Really? What is it this time - train was late so they offed the driver?"

Katz didn't even crack a hint of a smile.

"Nope, he's an investment banker in the city. They shoved him out in front of the train as it pulled into the station. Hundreds of witnesses and no-one saw anything."

"How do we know he was shoved? Maybe it was suicide? These places are a zoo at rush hour. It could have been an accident. Jeezo, it's always amazed me it doesn't happen more often."

"Yeah, I agree that would be a likely scenario, but there's another note. This time in the pocket of the victim. Brazen sonofabitches must have stuffed it in before shoving him off the platform."

"Holy shit! This is escalating. What the hell are they going to pull next?"

Katz put her hands on her hips.

"Well, I can give you a clue. How do you think your lanky friend got here? He's not likely to turn up for a bog-standard suicide now is he, sir?"

Stark pushed out his bottom lip and looked back toward Callahan. Heat flushed through his cheeks. Of course - the bad guys decided they needed more publicity for their cause. Callahan and the Daily News were perfect for them. They'd chosen the most popular hack, working for the nation's most popular paper: a paper renowned for championing the common man, bemoaning the decline of civilisation and generally stirring it for the authorities whenever they got the chance. Damn! Now the fun and games really would begin.

"Ah, shite. I better go see what he has to say for himself."

"Yeah, right you are, sir. I'm going to keep examining the scene if that's ok with you?"

Stark nodded and made to move away before realising his befuddled neurones were not linking up as they should.

"Wait, before I go over there...what does the note say this time?"

Katz handed over the evidence bag.

To whom it may concern,

I don't think my message is getting through.

Calvin here liked to shove little old ladies and pregnant women out of his way. Well, I gave him a push in the right direction. He learned a hard lesson in manners and what's right and wrong. I want them all to learn it. It's time to stand up against this tide of inconsideration and selfishness. It's time to reclaim the city for our decent, hard-working citizens. It's time to show respect.

Dwayne, Ernie and Calvin will help light the way.

Yours,

A concerned citizen taking action

There was something curious about this note. Instead of using a plain piece of paper like the others, it was printed on the back of what appeared to be a luggage tag bearing Calvin Jacob's personal details.

"What's with the luggage tag?"

Katz shrugged.

"No idea, sir. Strange huh?"

"Yeah, very," said Stark, handing the bag back to his partner. "Whoa! Wait a minute. Why is it all in the first person? There's no *we* or *us* in that statement - it's all *I* did this and *I* think that and it's signed off as *A* concerned citizen."

"Actually, yes, you're right, sir. So, what the hell was going on with Martin? Looks like his lush of a wife was talking through the bottom of her vodka bottle after all."

Stark pulled down on his jaw thoughtfully.

"Well, no, she wasn't as it happens. I checked out her story with the local plod and it turns out it's true. Martin did report being abducted and tied to the front of his truck by a couple of guys. The desk sergeant noted it, and a constable took a statement, but there was nothing more they could do. Martin had no idea where it happened and he never got a look at the two guys because they were wearing werewolf masks. The Sergeant actually thought he might have been making the whole thing up. He put it down to some kind of nightmare that seemed real or overindulging in home-brew."

Katz drew him a distinctly disapproving look.

"And you were intending on telling me this when, sir?"

"Yeah, ok, I'm sorry, Katz. I would've told you, it's just that, with everything that's been going on, I forgot, and right now it just became highly relevant," he replied slightly sheepishly.

His partner shook her head slightly and waved him off to speak to Callahan. Sometimes, Katz liked to act as if she was the senior officer. This would help her once that became a reality, in the meantime, he felt like a naughty schoolboy being dismissed by the headmistress. He summoned all his willpower in trying not to imagine Katz as the archetypal teacher in a porno movie, but he failed.

Back on the platform, Stark took Callahan by the elbow, leading him over to a pillar, out of the way of other cops and the rubberneckers being held behind the police cordon.

"Floyd, how did you find out about this?"

The big man tapped his nose again.

"Look, don't fuck about, Floyd. This is deadly serious. I don't have the time or the energy for games. How did you find out about this?"

Callahan actually looked wounded by Stark's curtness.

"Ok, Adam, sorry man, I was only pulling your dick. No need to be so bad-lieutenant about it. Sheesh!"

He pulled out his notebook and flipped to a page about three quarters of the way through it.

"I got a call at about seven this morning from a guy. Well, I say a guy, it sounded more like a computer. You know, like that scientist dude in the wheelchair - Stephen Hawkins or whatever his name is."

Stark nodded.

"Well, it just said to go to the station and ask the police how the guy on the tracks died. They guaranteed it wasn't suicide and he wasn't the first example they'd set."

Stark raised his eyes to the ceiling, waiting for the punchline.

"So, what's going on, Adam? We got ourselves a serial killer on the loose?"

And there it was.

"Floyd, we've known each other quite a while and you know I always help you when I can, right?"

"Yeah, and I'm always very grateful...so?"

"Well, this is a bit of a strange one. We're still at a very early stage and as you're all too aware, when we start linking crimes, the serial killer stuff can become a runaway train - if you'll pardon the pun."

They both smiled.

"Ok, Adam, but you know that the public have a right to know if they're in danger. So, what've you got and what way would you like me to play it?"

***

Stark was sure the arse-kicking for being a few minutes late had stopped but he was wrong. Off on the wrong foot again with his superior officer. A bad habit; must try harder.

"And another thing, I don't know how you used to do things in the land of haggis and neeps, but when you're working on a case from *my* station, I expect to be kept informed! Do you understand what that means, Stark?" shouted DCI Hargreaves.

"Yes, sir. I'm sorry, I'll make more effort from now on to involve you."

You racist twat, was the unspoken flourish Stark longed to add to the end of his reply. How his tongue remained in one piece while biting it so hard mystified him.

A huge emission of air rushed from DCI Hargreaves lungs, discharged via his nostrils. Stark felt under-prepared for the meeting, thinking perhaps he should have brought a three cornered hat and a red cape.

"Right, with luck, you've got that into your thick, Scottish skull. Now start talking!"

"Well, sir, so far, this is what we have. A young black guy called Dwayne Clements was abducted and mutilated about three weeks ago. The attacker left a note on Clements' person explaining their motivation as some sort of social crusade to improve respect and good manners. A drastic over-reaction to him spitting out his gum in the wrong place, apparently. Pulled out all his teeth and sewed up his mouth."

The DCI frowned deeply without interrupting, so Stark continued with his summary.

"Then, last week, we had a lorry driver called Ernie

Martin, from the Tower Estate, squashed between his truck and his van for the crime of tailgating. Looks like the same offender because they left a very similar note. They sign themselves off as a concerned citizen taking action."

"Well, they better be concerned when we finally catch up with them!" spat the DCI bitterly. "Go on, Stark. What else do you have?"

"The odd thing about this one is that the dead man's widow claims he was abducted and scared witless by *two* men a week before this fatal attack. Same idea, but like a warning of some sort, without the finality of murdering him. The local cops had nothing to go on and didn't take it very seriously. Looks like, with hindsight, they should have. However, we can't be sure how accurate the story is and all three notes are signed off in the singular, not the plural."

"Three notes? You've only mentioned two so far."

"Yes, sir, I was getting to that. This morning, we found victim number three; Calvin Jacobs. He's a city banker and was shoved in front of a Tube at rush hour. This time, the crime that riled our friend was Jacobs shoving people out the way on the Tube and being rude and aggressive."

"Him and ten million others!" quipped the Chief in a rare moment of levity.

The DCI got up from his chair and walked over to the window. The office sat many floors up, with an impressive view across their portion of the Capital. Hargreaves spoke with his back to Stark, hands clasped behind him; as if at ease on the parade ground.

"Are there any links between the victims or any forensics to work with?"

"No, sir, not yet I'm afraid. We're continuing to investigate whether the victims had any links, however tenuous, but so far we've not had any luck."

His boss slowly turned round to face him, folded his arms across his chest and fixed him with a look of utter contempt.

"Stark, police work has nothing to do with luck! It's about hard graft and putting in the hours. Somewhere there's a piece of evidence you've missed," a jabbing finger came out from the fold, "and I expect you to find it. I really don't need some sort of vigilante running around the city pretending to be the moral arbiter for us all. We decide who needs punished - not this guy."

"Yes, sir."

"Is that it?" barked Hargreaves, hands now thrust into his pockets.

"So far, sir. I'll let you know as soon as anything else develops."

"Yes, you will. That's all, Stark. You're dismissed."

16. THE MAGIC WORD

I already told you I hate trains. There are lots of reasons why but most of them are related to my fellow passengers' behaviour. I particularly hate the way people seem to forget they're sharing a small space with others: others who don't necessarily share their taste in music. Headphones are supposed to direct the sound into *your* ears, so *you* can listen to *your* music. They were not designed to be used on a one in and one out basis. The one in letting you enjoy whatever cacophony floats your boat, while the one out annoys the living crap out of everybody else within a ten mile radius.

This boy was about sixteen or seventeen maybe and the latest in a long line of annoying little faecal sacs I'd been forced to endure while taking train journeys. I suppose you might call him unlucky but, then again, you make your own luck in life don't they say? If he'd had the good sense to use his headphones in the way Mr Sony intended, he would have avoided my wrath, but he didn't.

This boy exuded a say-something-if-you-dare-old-man attitude. Dressed from head-to-toe in expensive sportswear, despite the minimal likelihood he'd recently darkened the door of any sports club or arena. Baseball cap worn with peak facing the rear: natch. This base-layer augmented with an array of tasteless, oversized jewellery and a face so acne-ridden it was hard to see any of his actual facial skin. His particular dose of this most distressing of teenage afflictions was so severe, it looked more like third degree burns than spots.

The choice of music player was a mobile phone, which blasted forth some god-awful racket by a rapper (one with a silent c as far as I could ascertain). He exacerbated this din by accompanying it with robust language, directed toward a video game contained within the same device. Apparently, he wasn't all that good at this particular game. The whole package was too irritating to let go. I decided to christen him Sports-boy.

I spent a good amount of time thinking about ways to get even with such anti-social scumbags on a number of recent trips. The plan I eventually devised depended on a certain set of factors to allow it to work. Those factors all came together on this journey, and I took my chance.

First, I needed to get close to the little turd in question, which I achieved easily enough. The aural pollution he cast into the atmosphere created an exclusion zone of at least two seats all around him. Sports-boy looked momentarily perturbed by the sudden proximity of a proper adult. Ordinarily, he would have no problem driving them away. After this initial disquiet, he soon re-assumed his arrogant 'screw-you-all' persona and returned to cussing vehemently in response to his gaming ineptitude.

The second element required for the success of my plan, depended on him being one of the aforementioned scumbags who preferred to leave one earpiece swinging free. Sports-boy duly obliged.

I stood up, snatched the phone from his grasp and made off down the carriage. He was too shocked at first to react. However, the round of applause and the whooping cheers of my fellow passengers soon shook him out of his torpor.

"Hey, you thieving motherfucker, give me my phone or I'll fuck you up real bad!"

If I didn't have something more pressing to attend to I

might well have spent the next twenty minutes laughing. His voice was so high-pitched it sounded like he borrowed it from a member of the audience at a Justin Bieber concert. Even if I didn't hold as many physical advantages over him as I did, that pre-pubescent outburst would not have induced any sense of foreboding in me.

As the carriage swayed and bucked, I carefully did what I had to do, then turned to face my accuser.

"Ask nicely and you can have it back."

"Fuck you, dickhead! I don't need to do anything you want - it's my phone. Now, give it back, before I call the cops."

"How will you call them, son? With your phone? Oh dear, that might be a little tricky," I replied, blatantly mocking him.

Poor little Sports-boy became very agitated but, now I was standing right in front of him, he realised he had no chance of intimidating me. The humiliation of being confronted and now taunted, burned like concentrated acid. However, even a retard like him could recognise conciliation was his only chance of getting his precious electronic friend back.

"Come on, man. Just give it to me!" he said as calmly as he could.

I shook my head and, as he made to grab, pushed him forcefully back.

"What's the magic word, sonny?"

This provoked a hilarious and totally unexpected response from the onlookers. A chant of "What's the magic word, sonny?" rose up, with every person on board joining in the chorus; all of them keen to encourage the boy to show some manners.

Sports-boy looked around in a fury that threatened to burst every zit on his face and shower us all with rancid, teenage pus. The impotence of his rage became clear to him as I effortlessly thwarted another attempted grab. The chant grew in volume and finally he acquiesced.

"Can I have my phone back...please?"

The final word whispered so as to be barely audible.

"I'm sorry, I don't think I caught that."

This time he screamed like a little girl.

"Can I have my phone back, PLEASE?"

The cheering, foot stamping and clapping was thunderous; a collective outpouring of relief, gratitude and schadenfreude. Finally, one of the unbearable few who made the lives of the many a misery had received their comeuppance. I don't mind admitting it made me feel good. This was not quite the end of it though.

"As you asked so nicely, yes, you can have it back. However, there is one condition."

He avoided my eyes and responded sullenly.

"What?"

"I want you to put both ear pieces in and turn down the volume. If you don't, I'll do more than just take it off you. Do you understand me?"

Again, he looked at the floor and mumbled, "Ok."

"I don't think I heard that."

"YES, OK!"

I handed the phone over but, as I did, I made sure he stuck to his promise and pushed the ear pieces into both ears for him. With a final, venomous glower, he took off up the carriage.

Almost immediately, we entered a station. The doors slid open, he alighted, and I returned to my seat. Much back-slapping and plaudits came my way but I kept my eyes on Sports-boy. Standing on the platform, he pulled at his ear pieces but they refused to budge. I saw him frantically looking back toward me as the train started to draw out of the station. He'd been left with no option but to stick to his promise - thanks to the super glue. I waved and gave him a salute.

Only now did I afford myself the luxury of laughing heartily. To be fair, I was laughing a lot less heartily than Garry, who was getting dangerously close to requiring oxygen or treatment for a hernia.

17. NIGHT-TIME

It's not always easy to relocate them, however, with a bit of effort, I usually succeed. This time it was the hospital helped me track him down. Although, to be fair on them, they were unaware of the aid they'd given me. Nonetheless, they had helped.

I never fail to be amazed at how extreme the lesson needs to be in order to get the message across. The earlier run-in and admonishment should have been enough of a warning to result in a permanent change of behaviour but, evidently, it wasn't. It's probably because he believed it was so unusual it could never happen again - after all, he'd gone unchallenged for so long prior to the train and the glue. It's also because that's the way people like him are, the way they were raised. They take no shit, they're an individual, with a right to express themselves in any way they see fit. Well, guess what, asshole? You're wrong! You're part of a society that needs you to follow some basic norms. These are things which help us all get along more smoothly, iron out the creases, prevent tensions overspilling.

He's wandering along with one ear in and one ear out.

Dissonance personified.

I'm wandering along after him. Both ears tuned in.

Righteousness personified.

PETER CARROLL

The place is ready to receive, even if he's not ready to give.

The dark surrounds me in it's welcome embrace. My senses are tuned in to every nuance, every whisper. Things that would unnerve others are absorbed and channelled.

I am very powerful now. Very, very powerful.

He would not have heard me without any aural distraction – in one ear or two. I think he'll listen from now on though.

The injection does its work admirably and, after a while, my lesson has been administered satisfactorily.

18. LISTEN UP PEOPLE

Along with the rest of my team, I was called to a briefing. A good number of beat cops were there, along with a few detectives. The usual eclectic collection of voices exchanging pleasantries, war stories, insults and jokes. Nobody seemed to know the purpose behind the gathering. I wandered over to Garry and discovered he was none-the-wiser either. We weren't kept in limbo for too long.

The prick that is Detective Chief Inspector Morris Hargreaves swanned in with his usual air of superiority and contempt, gesturing for us to take our seats. Once the hubbub subsided, he stepped to the front of the room.

"Ok, listen up, people. We have a vigilante or vigilantes running around this city and we need to start doing something to put a stop to their activities."

This was both intriguing and a total ball-ache. I could definitely kiss goodbye to the leave pencilled in for next week. This would be an all-hands-to-the-pump, overtime-fest.

Vigilantes are bad news for cops. If they choose the right cause, it can make us look like we're not doing our job properly. The man in the street often sides with them; positively roots for them even. Copycats come along and confuse the investigation. The switchboard overloads with hoax and crank calls and the press whip everyone up into a frenzy. Folks start carrying weapons to protect themselves and accidents happen as a result. Gung-ho civilians, intent on helping the cops, start wading into situations they'd be far better staying clear of. Nope, when all things are considered, as far as ordinary coppers are concerned, vigilantes suck - big time.

Now, detectives, that's a different matter - they love them.

Vigilantes tend to create complex puzzles which require piecing together carefully; most of them like to goad the cops regarding their inadequacies, so catching them is all the more satisfying; and with all the press coverage they normally get, the detective who solves the puzzle receives public recognition of their achievement, maybe even a promotion.

DCI Hargreaves relishes holding court like this. A big, juicy case to be solved is right up his alley. He looked particularly enthusiastic this morning.

"I'm going to hand over to DI Stark and DC Katz who will be leading the investigation and will get you up to speed with what we know so far."

Stark was a big guy, like me. Well-built, imposing and, if I wasn't a thoroughly heterosexual dude, I might even say handsome. Scottish: been in London for a while though, so the accent wasn't as thick as Taggart or Rab C. Nesbitt. Katz, on the other hand, was an out and out babe. Her incredible eyes were obvious from across the room, as were her dazzling, pearly whites. She has a kind of Latin look about her but I think someone told me she was English. Stark took the lead on filling us in.

"Thank you, sir. Good morning everyone. As DCI Hargreaves just said, we appear to have a vigilante on the loose. However, at this stage we can't rule out the possibility that there are two or more people involved."

A murmur sprung up, heads shook and sceptical glances were exchanged.

"Yes, I know, that's pretty unusual, but once you see where we're at, you'll understand why we can't totally discount it yet.

"It started with the assault of a young black man called Dwayne Clements. He had his teeth yanked out and his mouth sewn up for the heinous crime of...wait for it...chewing gum. More specifically, for not disposing of it appropriately. The attacker left a note explaining why they did it."

A few folks snorted with disbelief, a few 'no ways' were uttered, but Stark just carried on with the briefing. I was more than a little perturbed at how familiar that sounded.

"Next up, was a guy called Ernie Martin; white, poor, lorry driver. He got crushed between his truck and his van for being a tailgater. His wife says he was abducted by two guys and terrorised in a game of chicken a week before he was killed. Story checks out with the local plod - Martin reported it but the locals had nothing to work with. The problem we have here is that the note left at the scene of the murder is written in the singular. It makes no mention of a team effort."

I looked over at Garry, our eyes widening in unison. I shook my head to indicate that we should try not to draw any unwanted attention to our mutual anxiety. Stark went on.

"Then, last week, a city trader called Calvin Jacobs was shoved in front of a Tube train during the morning rush hour. This time the excuse given by our new hero was *Jacobs* shoved folks out of the way to get on trains, so he deserved it."

Again the muttering and gesticulations began to grow in volume and obviousness and Hargreaves felt compelled to intervene.

"Ok, people, let's settle this down shall we, and let DI Stark finish the briefing."

Reluctantly, the room came to order again.

"I know this all sounds a bit nuts. Frankly, it is. You could argue that whoever is responsible for these attacks is motivated by a sense of public duty. However, the extreme nature of the punishments handed out for the misdemeanours being committed, suggests mental imbalance. It also makes them very dangerous. If there *is* more than one perpetrator, then this case might veer even further from the beaten track.

"DC Katz and I set up an incident room and an evidence wall to track what's going on. I'd like you all to familiarise yourselves with it and keep your eyes and ears open while you're on the street. Somebody will know this person or persons and, sooner or later, they'll make a mistake and we'll get them."

A hand went up. Rob Kowalski, a good cop and a seasoned veteran, asked a good question.

"Do the press know about any of this?"

"Unfortunately, the bad guy or guys contacted Floyd Callahan at the Daily News and alerted him to their campaign. Me and Floyd go back a ways so, I asked him to lay off for now. But, you know journalists, they're under immense pressure to bring in big stories and this is a humdinger. I think we can safely expect the proverbial to hit the fan tomorrow.

"The problem is the public and the media will lap this shit up. The eye-for-an-eye brigade will love it, the liberals will be wringing their hands in angst over the rights and wrongs, and the TV and press will milk it for all it's worth. We can expect copycats and all the usual crap that goes with this kind of thing, so brace yourselves."

He was right but my brain accelerated into overdrive trying to work out what the hell was going on. I couldn't worry too much about what the right wingers or liberals might think. This was seriously messed up. I only ever did what I did as a warning, a shot across the bows. I was no vigilante, at least, I never thought of myself that way. I certainly wasn't conducting some kind of moral crusade. What really unnerved me was not that someone else clearly was, but that this someone else was evidently a big fan of my work. There was another issue; potentially much more problematic. If this guy got caught, he might well cite us as his inspiration. Sure, what me and Garry did was far less extreme, but if all the shit we'd been up to came out, we could kiss goodbye to our jobs, pensions, houses...families. I needed to keep abreast of this investigation without drawing attention to the fact I was unnaturally interested in it. Not only that, it would be far better for me and Garry if we found this sick motherfucker before he got the chance to implicate and incriminate us.

19. BACK IN THE GANG WITH A BANG

The gun felt reassuringly heavy in his hand. He turned it over and over, occasionally raising it and aiming into the mirror. In his mind's eye, a head rocked back, blood and brains showered the wall and his enemy folded like a Marionette whose strings were unexpectedly cut.

Looking in the mirror had become a painful experience for Dwayne. The scars were healing well enough, but he didn't have the money for decent dental work. As a consequence, the dentures he'd been fitted with were uncomfortable and irritating. So much so, that the pain drove him to remove them whenever he was in private. Without any teeth, his cheeks sagged inwards like those of a man four times his age. It made his speech laboured and indistinct and eating was a bit of a nightmare - this did not please him. These practical, physical difficulties were suffered in tandem with psychological issues. Dwayne became afraid of the dark, took to sleeping with a night light on. He never walked alone across the park any more and, whenever anyone crept up on his blind side, he found himself totally over-reacting.

When Dwayne got back from hospital he received a visit from some cops asking what happened, pretending they gave a shit; said they'd go after the twisted freak who did this to him...but he knew better. Dwayne amounted to less than nothing as far as they were concerned. Young, black, poor and all too familiar with the inside of their cells, and all too prone to be vocal in his displeasure at being incarcerated. No cop was going to help Dwayne get even. He'd be doing that himself.

His friends were shocked by what happened, offering to track the guy down and fuck him up. Dwayne was grateful for their support but that task was his. Just to be on the safe side, he enlisted the help of his best friend Lamar Stokes. They grew up together and Lamar was the only person in the world Dwayne trusted as much as his mother.

There was one major flaw in his plan though. Dwayne had no idea who his attacker was. In the toilet at the shopping centre, the guy made no attempt to hide his face, but in the park, he never saw him coming. In fact, he had no recollection of his abduction or mutilation whatsoever. Walking through the park one minute, the next, waking up in a hospital bed without any teeth. What angered Dwayne most was the trivial reason for these attacks. Spitting gum into a urinal for fuck's sake. He'd done some pretty bad things in his time - things which may well have merited some form of retribution from his victim - but *spitting out chewing gum in the wrong place*! It made no sense at all.

Dwayne only had one lead to go on - the shopping centre. He decided to stake the place out; maybe, just maybe, the piece of shit would turn up there and he would get his revenge. With no job and no effective parental control to interfere with his plans, he could afford to wait as long as it took.

It took about ten days. Luckily for him, the toilets had a bench outside; sufficiently far away from the entrance to avoid attracting unwanted attention but close enough to afford him a good view of the patrons. It's a tricky balance to strike conducting surveillance outside a public convenience. Staring too intently at the patrons might have provoked either of two unwanted reactions - sexual arousal or violent objection.

Dwayne almost missed the dude. Returning from buying a burger and coke, sipping through the straw that speared the lid on his enormous paper cup, he caught a glimpse of him as he went in. Even from behind Dwayne knew it was his man. The gait, the build, the get-up. Well, this time it would be Dwayne Clements who held the advantage of surprise and that huge motherfucker with the chewing gum issues was going to regret ever crossing him.

He dumped the remnants of the food and drink next to the bench, then he and Lamar crossed the concourse with purpose. Dwayne patted the small of his back, checking the gun was still there, even though he could feel the hard metal against his skin. He and Lamar had rehearsed what they were going to to do. Lamar would stand guard while Dwayne went in and capped the guy. Quick, easy, no messing, and then they'd be out of there. Lamar parked his motorbike close to the nearest exit and so, before anyone had time to react, they'd be gone.

Dwayne pushed at the door, looked up the length of the toilet. One guy using the urinals shook and zipped up. Dwayne gestured to him to get the fuck out of there. The guy was more of a boy and ill-equipped to forcefully object, so he did as he was told. Lamar, a giant of a man, with a string of convictions to his name, was more than capable of deterring any further intrusions.

Dwayne eased into the toilet, pulling the gun from his waistband as he did so. Sweat trickled down the small of his back, the gun damp, warm to the touch. For all the bravado he'd shown Lamar in the run up to this moment, he'd never even fired a gun, never mind killed anyone with one. This bastard deserved what was coming to him, but it didn't make Dwayne any less nervous.

He edged along, looking for a stall in use. The third in a row of six was the only one showing red on its lock. Dwayne took a deep breath. He could hear his quarry taking a dump. In normal circumstances, he wouldn't have taken any pleasure in listening to another man crapping.

However, it cheered him to think what a humiliating way it was to go - more humiliating than having your teeth pulled out and being left to look like your granddaddy's best friend.

Remembering how big the guy was and how easily he'd overpowered Dwayne previously, he decided to err on the side of caution.

"Alright, motherfucker! It's payback time. Let's see how you like chewing on these!"

With that, he unloaded the entire clip of ammo through the door of the stall. The noise was deafening, splinters of wood flew dangerously close to his face and by the time the eighth shot left the gun barrel, the door was hanging off its hinges. Dwayne stood, frozen to the spot, as the bloody carnage he'd wreaked was revealed to him. His ears rang, hands trembled uncontrollably. His heart beat so hard it felt like a pendulum banging back and forth between his sternum and spine.

Outside the door, Lamar kicked into survival mode. Before agreeing to accompany his friend on this mission, he got assurances it would be a quick, clean, efficient kill and they'd be out of there as soon as it was done. Dwayne, the stupid fuck, unloaded the whole clip, making an unholy racket in the process. People passing by stopped and stared at Lamar. He pushed the door open and saw Dwayne admiring his handiwork. Not moving.

"Yo, blood! Let's get the fuck outta here now! NOW!"

The scream jolted Dwayne into action. He jammed the gun back into his waistband and bolted for the door. The two of them raced for the exit, leapt onto the bike and roared off into the evening's rush hour traffic. Only once they were several blocks away, and convinced the cops were not on their tail, did Dwayne afford himself a victory whoop. He'd showed that fucker good and proper. He would return to the block a man again - a man to be reckoned with. A new reputation forged as a ruthless killer and a chance to put an end to the nicknames like Gums,

Grandpa and Grannyfucker.

***

The call came through while we were sitting in our car eating lunch. A shooting at the shopping centre but details were sketchy.

Me and Garry made our way to the toilets near the back. We were greeted by the head of security; a walrus of a man who introduced himself as Jackson Hodge. In an attempt to look officious and in charge he'd chosen to wear his cap. However, the company must have struggled to find one to fit a walrus and, as a result, the thing looked like he'd borrowed it from a passing child. I tried hard not to laugh.

"Hi, guys. Thanks for coming so quick."

I nodded.

"What you got for us, Jackson?"

"Got a dead, white guy in one of the stalls. Shot up real bad. At least six or seven bullets I reckon. Witnesses say they saw two black kids running away from the scene."

"Kids?"

"Well, teenagers, you know, youths. Not little kids if that's what you were thinking."

That was a relief but, these days, I tended to assume the worst and be glad to be proven wrong.

"Ok. Let's take a look then."

The area had been roped off using the kind of thing you see on a red carpet or opening ceremony. A couple of bored looking guards from Jackson's staff were preventing anyone crossing the temporary barrier. We ducked under the thick, red cord and made our way into the toilets.

The guy was indeed 'shot up real bad'. An impressive slick of blood pooled out from the stall, congealing on the floor. Shards of wood from the shattered door were strewn here and there. Excessive force was the phrase that sprung to mind. The smell of gunpowder hung in the air, mixing with faeces. Not the kind of eau de toilette you'd be thanked for giving to anyone as a Christmas present.

I looked at the guy's face. Interestingly, all the bullets which hit him, did so in the torso and legs; a couple clearly missed altogether and were embedded in the wall behind the cistern. Whoever our assassin was, he was no marksman. It was odd. I knew this dead guy, I was sure I knew him, but just couldn't place him.

"Garry, do you know this guy?"

"Nah, don't think so. Why? Do you?"

"No, probably just one of those things, you know, reminds me of someone I *do* know; their unknown double. What's that called again?"

"Doppelgänger."

"Yeah, that's it. Doppelgänger."

But it wasn't that. An icy knife of realisation ran me through as my memory connected the dots. This was the dude that came into the toilets after I'd made that boy Dwayne Clements swallow his gum.

Killers were black kids.

Shit!

This whole thing was getting more worrying by the minute. Why the fuck would Clements blow *this* guy away? He didn't do anything other than walk in at the climax of our little disagreement. Was I next? The little bastard had a gun and, manifestly, enough bottle to use it. My stomach fluttered, I felt adrenaline stream through my system.

It was important to stay cool. I couldn't give Jackson Hodge the impression I knew the victim, and giving any hint of knowing who was behind the shooting, would surely lead to the unravelling of my life. Keeping schtum was my only available option. There was no way to tell Hargreaves or Stark about my suspicions without

94

incriminating myself in relation to the original assault on Clements. That, in turn, would inevitably lead to accusations of being the vigilante. A quick mental audit revealed to me that I had no cover story, no alibi if that happened. I needed some head space.

"Garry, call it in, mate. MIT will need to deal with this now."

We walked back to the foyer outside the toilets and Garry duly reported in. It took about twenty minutes for the uniforms, detectives and SOCO to arrive. Once they were all briefed and reassured the area was safe, we escaped to a bar. A beer and a game of football on the TV sounded like just the distractions I required.

Sitting on a bar stool, allowing the alcohol to unwind the tension in my temples, I pondered the events of the day. It occurred to me it was more than likely Dwayne Clements would be caught quickly. CCTV cameras festooned the shopping centre, at least a dozen witnesses would identify him and his partner, and he'd been sloppy and careless to such a degree that his arrest was guaranteed without my intervention. I wouldn't need to get involved, I was certain of that.

I thought about the poor bastard who'd been shot and it made me feel awful. He'd probably used that toilet many times before. It was such bad luck he arrived in time for Clements to see him and assume he was in cahoots with me, which he wasn't of course. I wondered about his family and other unhelpful things which multiplied my feelings of guilt and complicity. I needed to stop drinking now or I was heading for a very dark and discouraging place.

I finished the beer, made my apologies to Garry, and headed home. Normality and love were calling loudly to me from my house.

20. CAN YOU HEAR ME NOW?

There it was, the beginning of the shit storm. As he walked past the news stand outside the Tube station, Stark noticed the Daily News headline blaring out across London and the rest of the world.

CITIZEN V!
Vengeance With Impeccable Manners

He reluctantly bought a copy - he really didn't want people thinking he was a regular reader or in any way sympathetic to the politics of this toilet paper with print on it. He felt like shouting out very loudly, "Don't worry, I'm a police officer and I'm buying this for purely professional reasons only! Nothing to see here, nothing to see here. Move along now, please!" Instead, he folded it so the logo would be obscured.

Callahan's report was predictably salacious and exaggerated. The approach of the editorial team at the paper was obvious: *of course* it didn't condone violence and murder, *but* all of us must have a secret admiration for the way this anti-hero was standing up for decent, hard-working folks who were sick of the spongers blah, blah, blah. The usual right-wing agenda they shoe-horned into any major story they covered. Knowing Callahan quite well, Stark found the politics of this rag at odds with the giant reporter's easy going, rather liberal, attitudes to life.

Then again, a crust needs to be earned; no doubt, a front page story like this one would keep Callahan kitted out with garish trainers for quite some time to come.

He did have to hand it to Callahan though. The name he'd given the vigilante was very good. It would provide endless hours of radio phone in fodder, chat show discussions and, for the more entrepreneurial out there, he could already see the clothing and other merchandising opportunities such a snappy moniker would present. Stark got on the Tube and made his way across town to convene with Katz and the Chief Inspector.

DCI Hargreaves was a seething mass of frustration and anger. He slammed the paper down on the desk in front of Stark and Katz.

"That is the worst of all possible worlds! A vigilante and a serial killer combined into one neat package, with the implicit backing of the most-read newspaper in the country. What I want to know, Stark, is how they got so much detail, so quickly? You assured me you'd had a word with your pal, Callahan. Well, I'd hate to think what he'd have written if you hadn't bloody bothered!"

His voice was raised but not at full volume. Hargreaves may only have been a small man in stature but he had a big impact on others.

"Well? What have you got to say for yourself, Stark?"

It was one of those can't win situations subordinates in any of the services often found themselves facing. They both knew nothing Stark said would earn him a reprieve but, by the same token, to actually say nothing and just take the bollocking would not suffice either. He could fight fire with fire and go down all guns blazing or he could acquiesce and slink away licking his metaphorical wounds. In truth, he couldn't be arsed fighting so acquiescence it was.

"Sorry, sir. I thought I'd...'

"Thought? You know what thought bloody well did,

don't you, son?"

It was a phrase that made no actual sense but was clearly understood by both parties to imply a lack of foresight on Stark's part. The DCI pressed his fingers together as if in prayer and tapped his chin, the skin on his face flushed, his blood pressure shooting skyward.

"Right, the cat's well and truly out of the bag on this now. The most important thing is to catch this idiot before he can cause any more problems for us. Do you think you're up to that, Stark?"

"Yes, sir."

"Yes, well, you better hope you are, son, because if this gets any worse, I'll be sending you back to Glasgow to hand out parking tickets. Do I make myself clear?"

"Yes, sir. Crystal."

It didn't take long for things to go from bad to worse.

"Ok, I'll let him know. We're on our way."

Katz put down the phone and gave Stark a look that he'd become very familiar with.

"Let me guess, another body, courtesy of our friend, Citizen V?"

"Not exactly, sir, but close. Something more like Dwayne by the sounds of it. Another mutilated youngster in hospital with no idea what happened to them."

"Great, the DCI's going to be so happy."

When they reached the hospital it quickly became apparent the press had been tipped off. A scrum of reporters, TV crews and radio journos, jostled and jockeyed for position outside the main entrance.

"Fuck! Drive around the block Katz and find somewhere to park away from the bloody vultures. I don't want to deal with them right now."

They parked the unmarked Mondeo a couple of streets away in a metered bay. Stark couldn't help thinking he might well be in charge of a few of those north of the border very soon.

"Do the honours will you, Katz. I've not got a scrap of change on me."

"You're like the sodding Queen you are, sir. Never seem to have any money on you. Scottish tightwad!" grumbled Katz.

"Watch it you or I'll have you cited for racial discrimination!"

Katz looked at him disdainfully and flicked him the bird before sticking enough money in the meter for a couple of hours parking.

Stark took out his mobile and made a call.

They walked into a yard at the back of the hospital where John Constance met them.

"Hi there, DI Stark, Detective Katz. Follow me."

The orderly was fit to bursting at being asked to aid Stark in his investigations. He led them to a door controlled by a swipe card and opened it with his accredited pass.

"Open says me!" he beamed, thinking his little joke to be highly amusing. No one else was particularly impressed. Certainly not Katz, whose skin crawled in the presence of Constance. He reminded her of a rodent with his furtive, darting eyes and pointed features. His horrible excuse for a moustache even looked like whiskers. She shuddered as she inadvertently brushed against him on her way through the door.

Stark shook the orderlies' proffered hand.

"Thanks, John. Really appreciate that, mate. Now, away back to work before someone notices you've gone. Don't want to get you into any bother."

"No worries, DI Stark. Always a pleasure to help you out, never a bother. Good luck - it's another weird one and no mistake."

Stark gave him another hand shake.

All Katz could muster was a cursory nod as she

accelerated away up the corridor. Stark half jogged after her and drew level as they turned a corner.

"Jings, Katz, you not so keen on my wee pal then?"

"He's a horrible, slimy, little rat. He gives me the bloody creeps!" she said with surprising vehemence.

"Aw, that's a bit harsh - he's just a lonely, wee, sad case that wants to feel important by helping the polis now an again."

"I don't give a shit, he creeps me out and, by the way, Jock, the word is police!"

He could have sworn she smiled as she said this.

"There you go again with that racialism. I'm going to HR to tell them I'm being oppressed!" He feigned a huff and they turned the next corner straight into Floyd Callahan.

"Starky! Imagine meeting you here!"

The beanpole reporter beamed his winning smile.

"Don't you Starky me you lanky git! I take it your pal Captain V sent you a message? Shone a spotlight into the night sky - the V signal was it? Well here's a V signal from me you prick!" and with that, Stark delivered a two-fingered salute.

"Detective Inspector Stark, that's very hurtful, as well as being more than a tad rude. It just so happens that *Citizen* V did indeed tip me off about his latest exploits. Not been able to get into the room though, thanks to a half pitbull, half ward sister guarding the door," came the jovial reply.

Katz snorted.

"If you two are quite finished, perhaps we could go and check on the victim...*sir*?"

"You see that, Callahan? That's what the modern police force is like nowadays. No bloody respect any more!"

Katz had walked ten yards, showed her warrant card to the guard dog/sister and stepped into the room before Stark had even finished his sarcastic riposte. He just shrugged, smiled at Callahan and followed after her.

As Stark closed the door behind him, he took in the scene. A young, uniformed, female constable was handing over an evidence bag to Katz, bringing his partner up to speed in hushed tones. A boy of about seventeen lay in the bed, head swaddled like an Egyptian Mummy, awake but looking very sorry for himself. He was hooked up to a couple of pieces of equipment that whirred and beeped intermittently. A frumpy-looking, middle-aged woman, who Stark assumed was the boy's mother, sat on a chair, stroking his forearm tenderly. A lump of sodden paper tissue protruded from the sleeve of her blouse and she pulled it out and dabbed at her nose as she sniffed.

Katz dismissed the young cop and she and Stark both turned their attention to the mother.

"Hello, Ma'am. I'm Detective Inspector Adam Stark and this is Detective Constable Lara Katz. I'm sorry to intrude but we really need to speak to your son about what happened to him."

She struggled to control her emotions, her lip quivered and tears and snot began to slip down her face.

"Please catch the animal that did this. My poor, beautiful boy..."

She tailed off as sobs prevented her actually speaking coherently, the paper tissue saturated beyond helping to remove any of the additional moisture she was producing. Luckily, Stark always attended such situations with a packet of disposable handkerchiefs in his pocket. Experience taught him this was helpful on a number of levels - not least of which was winning the trust of victims and letting them know he actually gave a crap about their trauma. He passed her the packet and she nodded gratefully as she took them; emitting a surprisingly powerful noise as she blew her nose.

"Sir, this is Mrs Pritchard and that's her son, Luke. He was attacked on his way home from a party at one of his friend's houses. He didn't see the attacker and has no recollection of anything that happened after he left the party. Whoever attacked him," Katz surreptitiously made a V with her fingers in order to confirm to Stark that this act belonged to their man, without alarming or alerting Mrs Pritchard, "cut off his ears, then dumped him a couple of streets away from here, where a passerby found him and called an ambulance. The constable said the doc told her he'd been sedated but also had alcohol in his bloodstream as well as traces of cannabis."

Mrs Pritchard's face suddenly hardened and she gave her son a stare that needed no augmenting with words.

"Ok, let's just forget about lectures and so on as far as his social life is concerned for now," said Stark. "We'll leave all that to you for later, Mrs Pritchard. What I want to know, Luke, is what you remember. Just start at the beginning and give me everything you can."

The boy looked broken - physically and emotionally - struggling to come to terms with what happened to him. A sudden thought occurred to Stark.

"Sorry, can you actually hear me ok, Luke?"

Luke nodded slightly.

"Good, sorry, it's just...you know..."

Stark felt a bit foolish at this outburst.

"Go on, Luke. Tell us what you can," interjected Katz.

"I don't really remember anything," came the whispered reply.

"Start with the party. Who was there? When did you leave? That sort of thing. Sometimes a tiny thing can really help us," Katz suggested softly.

Stark really liked this modulation. There was a hint of a foreign accent in Katz's voice that served to make it sexy; despite the serious nature of the words being spoken.

It didn't have that effect on Luke, if anything, it seemed to increase his nervousness and unease.

"It was my friend Ryan's party."

"Do you have a phone number and address for Ryan?" Stark asked.

"Yeah, he lives on the next estate to us, 10 Pheasant Avenue. You can find his number in my phone."

Katz picked up the phone and scrolled through the contacts until she reached an entry called Ryan. Luke confirmed the number belonged to his friend and she scribbled the number on her notepad, then placed the phone back on the bedside table.

"Go on," prompted Stark.

"His Mum was away so he had the house to himself. There was a whole bunch of people there but I didn't know that many of them. I got bored and left about midnight. I was walking home coz I can't afford taxis and it wasn't that far..."

He drifted away and his eyelids began to droop.

"I think that's enough for now, Detective Inspector. He's very tired and full of painkillers. He already told the policewoman who was here earlier all that he knows, which seems to be very little," said Mrs Pritchard, springing to her son's aid despite her disapproval of his flirtations with illegal herbs.

Katz and Stark exchanged glances. She was right. There was little to be gained by pushing hard right now.

"That's fine, Luke. You need to rest and get better as quickly as you can," Stark said sympathetically.

"Bye for now, Mrs Pritchard. We'll come back when he's feeling stronger."

21. LION HUNTING

I was sitting in the spare room noodling on my guitar. The room's a half-hearted attempt at a home-studio. A musician since my early teens, I played in a succession of bands that never really got anywhere. These days, I express my muse through Cubase, composing little ditties via the computer that no-one other than my son's goldfish would be interested in. And, let's be honest, the fish only tolerated them because it couldn't remember how shit they were between each listening. I also filled some time posting video tutorials on YouTube for kids to learn how to play their favourite rock tracks. It's important to put something back. Actually, more like a pathetic attempt to try and prove to the world that I still had it, which I never did. Still, at least I could recognise my own shortcomings - even if I couldn't avoid them.

Browsing YouTube as I doodled on the fretboard, I looked for stuff on this Citizen V character, trying to find out who this fucker was. Why was he following me, upping my ante and 'finishing off' what I started?

When I stumbled upon the video, the blood in my veins seemed to thicken and solidify as I watched. A disturbing, grinding noise turned out to be coming from my teeth and my eyes widened to the saucer proportions of a cartoon character.

I should have bloody-well known better. Stupid, arrogant, dick. I'd gotten away with my exploits so often that I became blasé, undercooked my preparations and failed to think through scenarios.

The video was entitled 'What's the magic word sonny?'. Someone on the train took out their smartphone and videoed my exploits once the crowd started singing the eponymous refrain. I should have waited for a one-on-one situation! What was I thinking about conducting my business in front of an audience? Hubris, that's what did it. I mean, what the actual fuck was I going to do about this?

I could try and track down the person who posted it, find some way to persuade them to delete it. Shit idea. The fucking thing had already scored four hundred likes and been shared sixty-five times. Fingers crossed, no-one who knew me would find it before I could sort out some kind of plan.

If a cop or one of the MIT team got onto this I would have to answer a whole shitpile of difficult questions. Clements would identify me for sure, I never made any attempt to hide my face from him. The lorry driver might be dead, but me and Garry definitely abducted and scared the living crap out of him, before this Citizen V murdered him. With enough effort and the right motivation, the forensics guys would likely discover some minute scrap of incriminating evidence to confirm that. Witnesses might have seen me trip Jacobs, particularly when prompted with photos of me: the woman who walked past, for instance. If I didn't have an alibi for the time he was killed...

I scrolled down the comments and my heart stopped. Not metaphorically. It *actually* stopped, along with my breathing, vision and any sense of perspective. I was fucked. Well and truly shafted!

Fifteen comments down, someone called Moondogvomit666 proclaimed:

'I no this fucker! Hes a copper. Arested me once. Works out of Hackney. Citizin Vagina - a total cunt!'

Replies alternating between 'LOL!' and 'bullshit!' followed on.

There were two saving graces. Moondogvomit666, whoever he was, failed to name me explicitly and, since his post, many more comments followed on. As a result, his revelation was hidden four pages back. It really needed looking for, so this might buy me some time.

Why hadn't I thought of a phone? I made sure the train didn't have any CCTV on board but patently failed to think about the rest of the modern world. It's not as if I'm some kind of technophobic Luddite. I use this technology myself every day. I know my way around a computer and I've got an iPhone for god's sake. Hubris. Fucking hubris, that's what did it.

I needed to think, to get out of the house. I shouted to my wife that I was going out to get a few beers to drink with the game later.

Driving out into the early evening, my mind spun web after web of possibilities. The streets were filled with people oblivious to my predicament and I tried to think how I might escape it.

***

Bobby 'Bubba' Harvey found working for the Corantelli family to be a pretty satisfying experience. Sure, Leo could be a bit of a dick at times but it was easy to ignore his petulance for what it was. In general, they treated him well, paid handsomely and allowed him to enjoy the status and violence that came with his role.

Bubba spent years working as a doorman. He gained Carlo Corantelli's attention one evening while dealing with some particularly unpleasant drunks in a very forceful but controlled manner. The club involved happened to be Carlo's most prestigious and it mattered that such things were handled appropriately. Very soon Bubba graduated to Chief of Security for Leo.

The incident in Cardoza's tarnished his reputation with the old man a little. Leo was ok about it. After all, he ordered Bubba to 'kindly fuck off and leave him alone' that night. To be fair, Bubba was pretty sure if he'd been screwing the girl Leo picked up that evening, he'd like some privacy to do so. Leo also didn't make too much fuss in an attempt to ensure no-one found out exactly what happened in the toilets. Leo wasn't aware, but he'd failed. Everyone in the team looking after him knew about the phone's rectal insertion. In fact, they even coined a new nickname for him as a result - "Ring Ring" - as in, if you need to call him, ring his ring. The drunken game of cards where this nickname arose proved impossible to finish once Barry Kennedy came up with it. Bubba thought he might actually die he laughed so hard.

Bubba didn't usually spend much time on the internet but tonight he wanted to browse for clues. Various bits and pieces caught his attention but, aside from the unclothed women, the most interesting clip was on YouTube. It showed some everyday citizen, vigilante-type guy facing up to a teenager on a train and confiscating their mobile phone. He scrolled through the comments for a few pages and found a very interesting snippet from a brainless muppet called Moondogvomit666. The possible link with Leo's attacker seemed promising. He took a screen grab and printed it off.

An hour later, he stood in the alley behind Cardoza's with a very nervous Myles Gilmore quivering in front of him.

"Is this the guy who attacked Mr Corantelli?"

The print of the video was grainy, indistinct, but Myles knew right away it was his customer. The moral dilemma facing him was one he desperately hoped he'd never need to face. If he said yes, the guy might end up being killed in some heinous fashion. That, in turn, might end up with him getting into trouble for helping the criminals in their task. If he said no and, subsequently, Corantelli found out he'd been lying, Myles himself might end up as worm food.

'Err, I, err..'

Bubba put a rather hefty paw on Gilmore's shoulder. "Don't make me force you to make up your mind, son. Is it him?"

"Yes," whispered Myles.

"Thanks. See you later and, remember, I was never here, right?"

Myles nodded. As Bubba walked away down the alley, Myles rushed over to a bin and threw up.

***

Leo Corantelli looked at the screen on his phone as it lit up and the ringtone bleeped out. The tune was irritating and the number displayed unrecognised as a stored contact. This was not so surprising given it was a new mobile. Considering where it had been lodged, he couldn't bear to keep using the old one - despite it being perfectly serviceable after its adventures in his lower digestive tract. He decided to take the call. With any luck it would be in regard to the bastard responsible for his proctological assault. At the very least it would bring a halt to that infuriating jingle.

"Hello?"

"Leo, it's Bubba. I think I found the guy you're looking for."

"He better hope not!" replied Leo bitterly.

"You're not going to believe this - I'm pretty sure he's a cop!"

Leo almost crushed his new phone in anger and outrage.

"A fucking cop? You're shitting me right?"

Leo failed to notice the ironic and slightly inappropriate colloquialism and Bubba felt it best not to mention how funny he found it. Ring ring.

"Nope, I shit you not. He's based right here in the city and I know exactly where to find him," Bubba said with a certain air of pride in a job well done...and a smirk for a joke well concealed.

"OK, get over here, now!"

"On my way, boss."

Leo cancelled the call, popped the phone back in his pocket. He looked down at his desk, various bits of paper adorning it. All of this mundane admin could wait until the much more pressing matter of the cop was expedited. The past few weeks had been very difficult to bear. The hunt for his attacker proved to be trickier than he thought it would be, but now he realised why.

A cop. He could hardly believe it. Sure, he'd been on the receiving end of some rough treatment from the cops in his time, but always in relation to some investigation or arrest. To be assaulted in public like that was humiliating enough, but by an *off-duty* cop? That was just salt in the wound. Saying that, he almost admired the guy; to have the cojones to attack someone like him either took huge bravery or huge stupidity. The only other option would be that this was the one cop in the city who didn't know who Leo was. However, this fucker of a cop would soon become very well acquainted with Leo Corantelli - it just wouldn't be in any way he'd find gratifying. Bravery, stupidity or ignorance; it didn't really matter to Leo which option drove the cop's thinking. All that mattered was making sure he regretted ever acting upon those thoughts.

Leo pulled out the drawer of his desk, reached for the old phone. He'd only listened to the message once but the smarmy, self-satisfied tone, the insulting words, burned into his memory. He put it in a pocket separate from the new one, walked over to the safe, spun the combination and opened the door. Taking out his gun, ensuring it was loaded, he tucked it into the waistband of his trousers in the small of his back. He also picked up the flick knife; automatically opening then closing it again. It went into a custom-made holster attached to his calf, concealed under his trouser leg.

Making his way to the front door, Leo donned a heavy overcoat, wrapped a scarf around his neck and stepped out onto the wide, gravel driveway that swept up to his impressive abode. The chill air nipped at the top of his ears and the tip of his nose. There was a change in the seasons afoot. He pulled on his gloves as Bubba coasted into the driveway, gravel crunching under the tyres of the BMW. His Chief of Security got out without killing the engine and opened the back door for him. Leo settled into the leather upholstery and thought dark thoughts of revenge.

"Bubba."

"Yes, boss?"

"Take me to this cocksucker, right now!"

No further encouragement was required. Bubba accelerated out of the driveway and onto the street. Leo's hunt was almost complete.

22. IDENTITY CRISIS

Dwayne Clements sat in his chair in the interview room looking pretty sorry for himself. His head rested on the backs of his hands on the table-top and an untouched, styrofoam cup of tea beside him had gone cold.

The cops picked him up in the early hours of the morning. A review of the CCTV footage at the shopping centre showed him and Lamar Stokes leaving on the motorbike. It was fair to say Lamar and Dwayne were not really intellectually cut out for a life of crime. Not only had they been filmed but Lamar used his own bike, and failed to cover the registration plate. A very small amount of elementary police work led the MIT straight to them.

They'd both been dragged in and spent the last four hours stewing in cells. Lamar, uncooperative, surly, determined to hold out and give the pigs nothing. Dwayne, on the other hand, bricking it. All the bravado and swagger he'd shown his crew on the estate drained out of him in the cell. He'd not even bothered to ditch the gun; the cops found it under his mattress after the most cursory of searches. His mother collapsed in shock when she saw it. He felt really bad about that. She was a good woman, tried her best to raise him well in very difficult conditions. He knew there was no way out of this. He was going down for a long, long time.

Dwayne couldn't help but feel hard done by. Why him? Why had the sick bastard decided to pick on him for spitting out his gum in the toilet? Thousands of people did that every day; was this fucker out there stopping all of *them* by pulling out their fucking teeth? At the time, it felt good to vent his anger via the gun but that victory seemed pretty hollow now. Jail beckoned and, when he got there, he could look forward having his skinny, little, black butt relentlessly invaded. Acting tough was one thing - being tough was quite another. He let out a slight sob as a solitary tear dropped onto the floor below the table.

Stark watched through the one-way glass, sipping coffee and thinking how an already unusual case had just become even more peculiar.

Dwayne Clements was accused of murdering a middle-aged plumber called Tony Stout. According to witnesses and camera footage, Dwayne and his pal Lamar Stokes, cornered Stout in the toilets of a shopping centre, shooting him four times. Forensics reported eight shots in total but it appeared Dwayne could do with some time on the practice range. The sergeant sent to pick them up recognised Clements' name from the briefing and contacted Stark to let him know he was about to be arrested. The DCI authorised Stark to do the interviews; even though no-one knew yet whether or not the shooting had a direct link to the Citizen V case.

The team who picked them up described Stokes as being rude, aggressive, defiant, whereas Clements acted quiet and nervous; bordering on timid. It made sense to go to Clements first, then deal with Stokes afterwards.

"Katz?"

"Yes, sir?"

"Has the duty solicitor turned up yet?"

"I think I saw her a minute ago, sir."

"Right, in that case, let's get in there and have a wee word with Mr Clements."

Stark thought Dwayne looked awful. The sunken cheeks

and scars, added to his dishevelled clothing and bloodshot eyes, made him look like a fifty year old wino rather than an eighteen year old boy.

The duty solicitor was an old stager called Eleanor Gamble. Stark admired and respected her. Unlike the usual cynical cows or rookie numpties poor sods like Dwayne could normally expect to be allocated, she still cared about doing a good job; trying to acknowledge the smallest ounce of decency buried deep within the most despicable of clients. This did not make her a soft touch though. She had a fantastic way of preventing her clients from swamping cases with oceans of bullshit. By the same token, the cops were not allowed free rein to do as they pleased in pursuit of their version of the truth.

"Hi, Eleanor. How are you today?" asked Stark.

"I'm ok, thanks, DI Stark. Nice to see you again, and you, DC Katz."

His partner nodded and smiled rather thinly. For some unknown reason, Katz did not appear to be all that enamoured with Eleanor Gamble. Stark thought Katz could do with a spell in charm school.

Stark pressed the tape machine to start recording the interview. Such an arcane and clunky thing to be using, but considered more secure and less easy to doctor than the digital alternatives.

He reeled off the usual introductions, caveats and scene setting required for the record, then addressed Dwayne directly.

"Dwayne, why did you shoot Tony Stout dead in that toilet?"

Eleanor Gamble raised her eyebrows at the bluntness. Stark was not one to waste time with niceties.

The boy just shrugged and looked at the table.

'So, you're not denying it then?'

Again the shrug.

"Dwayne, you need to speak, son. This is a tape recorder and shrugging won't be enough if it gets played back at a later date. Did you shoot and kill Tony Stout?"

"Yeah, if that's the geezer's name, I shot him," came the rather quiet reply.

"Do you mind telling me why, son?"

"He's the motherfucker that pulled my teeth out. He fucking asked for it, man. Ok!" This time he shouted the reply.

Stark, Katz and Gamble were taken aback by this sudden, forceful revelation.

"Sorry, Dwayne, you're saying Tony Stout was the guy who assaulted you?"

"Yeah, man! He's the fucker and I sorted him - good and proper like!" Dwayne was beginning to enjoy venting his ire.

"Right, interview suspended at 11.30am. We'll continue this in a wee while. Is that ok with you, Eleanor?"

"Yes, I have another client to sit in with, so I'm not going anywhere else anyway."

Katz and Stark convened in the hallway.

"What do you think?" Stark asked.

"Not sure, sir. Sounds a bit implausible. I spoke to Tony Stout's boss and he said the guy was married with two small kids, wouldn't say boo to a goose. They were all devastated and couldn't understand why anyone would want to kill him," Katz replied.

Stark needed to stop looking so intently into her eyes. He was becoming ever so slightly aroused and that would not do at all.

"Yeah, but who knows what kind of person this Citizen V is. They seem to have some sort of moral compass or social conscience thing going on. Maybe they would seem perfectly normal to the folks around them?"

"That's a good point, sir, I suppose. It's just, I don't know...in my head, I don't have a plumber as the person writing those notes and doing those violent things all over the city."

The two of them paused to think and digest what was going on.

"I need you to do a bit of digging on this Tony Stout guy. See if we can put him somewhere other than the scenes. If it was impossible for him to have done any of them, I think we need to talk to Dwayne again and see if we can get a bit more out of him."

"Ok, sir. I'm on it. I'll get back to you as soon as I can."

Stark watched her go off up the corridor and through a set of double doors. His eyes never left her arse the whole time.

***

Lara Katz's parents were Bosnian immigrants; refugees from the civil war that tore Yugoslavia apart in the early 1990's. They brought nothing with them other than the clothes they wore, their daughter and some bitter memories. Her father, an eminent professor of history, was eternally grateful that the academic world of London embraced him when he needed them most. Within a few years they were living in relative comfort again, although always restless, talking of when they would return to their old home.

Lara had been a toddler when she arrived in the UK and remembered nothing of the land of her birth. Raised and schooled in London, she was bilingual, which accounted for the hint of an accent when speaking in English. A few family members lived in Sarajevo and she'd visited a couple of times since her late teens. Three months ago her parents finally found the resolve and the money to go back. Without siblings, she was alone in the big smoke. However, it didn't bother her much, she'd always been independent and resourceful.

Police work suited Lara. She was tenacious, inquisitive and intelligent, as well as fearless; mentally and physically. The manner in which her parents were forced to flee their homeland definitely helped draw her to a job involving upholding law and order. Justice seen to be done.

Lara was one of a few rising stars identified by the Met for fast-tracking into senior positions. Her appointment to work with Adam Stark in MIT was part of this training process; designed to see her ready to sit the exams and become a Detective Inspector within two years. As a woman, and a very attractive woman to boot, she needed to battle all manner of prejudice and assumptions about the process. Most young cops accepted it as part of the way things were and knew no different. However, a lot of the older guys - and they were almost always guys - had a distinct chip on their shoulder about it. She developed a thick skin and selective hearing, just got on with it. Her morose persona was part of this coping mechanism. She decided early on in her career, if she was too sunny or chatty, it might just reinforce the misogyny of the cretins who indulged in such behaviour.

Stark seemed a decent boss as far as she could tell: even-tempered, could take a joke as well as dish it out, and treated her with respect in front of others. There were times when she felt he might be checking her out, but it was subtle, nothing that made her feel uncomfortable. As long as Lara didn't encourage him, he seemed to know where to draw the line professionally. All in all, she could have been lumbered with a lot worse for a partner and mentor. Stark was also a damn good cop, which would hopefully mean looking good by proxy and getting the promotion she craved.

This case was a real teaser. A case that, if they managed to solve it, would gain them a great deal of recognition within the MIT. No, there was no *if*. They *would* solve it. She was sure that between her and Stark they would muster enough brain power and determination to get there.

Katz spent the next hour or so checking with Tony Stout's wife and boss on his whereabouts at the times of the attacks undertaken by Citizen V. If they were to be believed, and there was no compelling reason not to believe them, the good Mr. Stout was just that; there was no way he was Citizen V. She thanked the two witnesses and relayed the news to Stark.

Returning to the interview room, they found themselves armed with a rather different set of questions to the ones they imagined asking earlier that morning.

Dwayne was seated at the table again, with Eleanor Gamble by his side. Stark and Katz sat opposite them and Stark once again performed the obligatory formalities in terms of the tape.

"Dwayne, you told us earlier that Tony Stout attacked you. Is that right?"

"Yeah, man. That's what I said, innit."

The reply was more surly and downbeat than before. Perhaps some more time in his cell had cooled his jets a touch; thinking of his future or lack thereof.

"Hmm. That's really interesting Dwayne because at the time you were having your teeth pulled out, Tony Stout was in a pub full of his friends and family celebrating his fortieth birthday."

The look that crossed Dwayne's face was a mixture of disbelief and dismay.

"What do you mean, man? It was him. I saw him. He was the one what attacked me. I don't care what his homeys said - he attacked me, he wasn't at no party!"

"Dwayne, there are at least thirty witnesses who can vouch for him. His wife told us his brother and another friend needed to carry him up to his bed he was so drunk. He didn't attack you Dwayne, so tell me why you really killed him."

Dwayne trembled, fidgeted and muttered under his breath, building up a head of frustrated steam. Stark could practically hear the cogs turning in the boy's mind as he desperately tried to come up with a new story.

"I..." as nothing came to him, the frustration fizzled out. "I..."

Katz abruptly interjected.

"Dwayne, can you just explain something to me? You told the doctors that you never saw your attacker. You were drugged and unconscious. How could you possibly know that Tony Stout was the man that attacked you?"

Dwayne squirmed in his seat and Eleanor Gamble looked at him in sudden realisation that she'd failed to notice this flaw in his story.

"Well? How?" Katz insisted.

"He was in the toilet at the shopping centre the first time, ok! He made me eat piss-covered gum, man! I mean, it was fucking disgusting, man!"

The detectives exchanged glances and Stark rejoined the interrogation.

"The first time, Dwayne? What do you mean? You never mentioned that you'd been attacked twice. When did this happen?"

"It was a couple of days before the teeth thing. Big white dude, pulled a gun on me, then forced me to eat a bit of gum I spat in the bowl when I was taking a piss. Kept going on about manners and how it wasn't the attendant's job to clean up after me. He was one sick motherfucker but I showed him! I got me my own gun. I knew he'd come back there eventually and when he did, I capped his white ass good and proper, man!"

Stark took a moment to process this. It was important to nail down exactly what was going on.

"Sorry, let me get this right, Dwayne. You're telling me that Tony Stout pulled a gun on you in broad daylight, in a public toilet? Then, he made you swallow some gum you'd spat out into the toilet bowl?"

"Yeah, man, that's what I'm telling you. That's what happened, man."

Katz was also processing fast.

"Still makes no sense, Dwayne. We just told you Tony

Stout has witnesses, and probably photos if we asked for them, proving he was somewhere else when you were attacked the second time. Was he alone? Did he have an accomplice?"

Dwayne began dredging his memory. The drugs Citizen V administered played havoc with his recollection of the attacks. He was sure Tony Stout was in the toilet. He was *definitely* the guy who put the gun to his head...wasn't he? With each beat of his heart, Dwayne's blood seemed to carry another batch of doubt to his brain. Confusion clouded his mind. A sudden flashback. Two men.

"There were two of them, yeah. That's right. He was the one with the gun though, the other dude just came in when he..."

Stark looked at Katz and they both looked at Eleanor Gamble.

"I think we should stop there, DI Stark. I urgently need to talk to my client."

Stark suspended the interview. It was now clear that, although Tony Stout was very much dead, Citizen V was still very much alive.

23. SUSPICIOUS MINDS

Abby Hester looked in the mirror and dabbed the last of her foundation on. Though she said so herself, she was a good looking woman. A good looking woman with a life going very well at the moment.

The private medical practice in Harley Street she joined a year ago was booming. It amazed her how many rich folks were feeling insecure about their looks. Still, she couldn't complain; every imperceptibly crooked nose straightened, and every perfectly normal chest expanded, in turn expanded her bank account. The young Abby, full of principles, working to make the world a better place, used to be very snooty about this sort of thing. But, years of having her emotions and sympathy chipped away, in order to survive the horrors of what life threw at her patients, took their toll. She no longer worried about such lofty ideals.

She moved into the flat a couple of weeks ago and it was impossibly lovely. Two large bedrooms, a beautiful aspect across the park and loads of delightful period features. The Aston Martin was an 'extravagant, bloody indulgence' but she couldn't care less what her father thought; she adored it. Well, what the hell, no kids and a six figure salary plus bonuses. She couldn't take it with her.

Her love life was looking up too.

The wine bar was one the unattached girls and boys from the practice liked to go to at the end of a long week's cutting and sewing. On the evening in question, as busy as ever; getting served involving extended periods standing with a ten pound note in your hand, waving it in a vain attempt to attract the attention of the staff.

He'd used a pretty good 'crap' chat-up line.

Pressed against the bar, amongst the heaving mass of thirsty punters, Abby hadn't noticed him moving up beside her.

"Gorgonzola."

"What?"

"Sorry, is that too cheesy?"

A knockout smile, tall, handsome, well dressed. He smelled good too. What more could she want? She couldn't help but laugh. He offered to buy her a drink and, by the end of the evening, he'd come twice. She'd come so many times she'd lost count and almost lost consciousness.

The passion and adventure of their sex was incredible. They'd done things she'd only ever read about in novels; including a threesome. She could tick that off the bucket list but made it clear to him it was a one-off. He, of course, pestered her for a repeat on a regular basis.

One major issue marred things; his marital status.

Abby never planned this, never thought she'd end up being 'the other woman' but nonetheless, here she was. However, with Abby behind him, he would gain the courage to leave his awful wife, she was sure of it. Patience - she loved him and he loved her. It would all work out ok. Abby was going to win.

***

Garry Black loved being a copper. There were lots of crap things about the job for sure but, ultimately, he could park them in a corner of his mind. Nothing compared to the power trip when he collared some little turd in a tracksuit for attacking a pensioner or some junkie wanker helping himself to a shop-keeper's profits. The adrenaline-infused thrill of driving at ridiculous speeds with total impunity took some beating. And, talking of beating, he absolutely loved when things got physical; it was a matter of personal pride that he'd never been felled in the line of duty. That despite plenty of big (and little) fuckers having a bloody good go.

He'd worked in a variety of stations across London but liked working in Hackney the best. Yes, the place was challenging and a lot of the clientèle left something to be desired, but it was never dull. One of the main reasons for enjoying his job so much in recent times was his promotion to work in the Specialist Crime and Operations Directorate or SCO19 as it was known. Racing round town in a Trojan, bristling with guns, was the stuff of every small boy's fantasy. His latest partner was a good guy. Unfortunately, Garry's wife didn't like Steve much. She thought him a bad influence but they had a laugh and a similar outlook on life. What mattered most in such a perilous occupation was having a partner you could trust to watch your back. Steve was that guy, so his wife's misgivings were irrelevant. Armed Response was a dangerous job and the training tough but worth all the effort. It certainly knocked being a beat cop into a cocked hat. The job also brought with it prestige, earning them kudos and sour envy in equal measure.

The revenge stuff amused Garry. Although, he did think most of what Steve suggested ended up being pretty tame. Garry managed to persuade him to up the ante a bit for the trucker, which was fun. What happened after was unfortunate but he'd not lose any sleep. The guy just wouldn't take a telling; he deserved it. One less dangerous arsehole on the road to worry about. Getting caught worried him though. Steve was right about keeping a low profile at work regarding the case. There was no point being unnecessarily bold about such things; after all, it would definitely threaten his freedom and he really didn't like the idea of being an ex-copper in prison.

***

It came to me as I drove; on the evening I saw the YouTube footage. It suddenly seemed so obvious. I couldn't understand why it hadn't occurred to me earlier. Garry!

He knew all about my revenge schemes; hell, he was there when several of them were taking place. He chastised me regularly for not going far enough, for being a pussy, letting them away with such minor punishments. He had the opportunity and the information it would take to go after all of my victims and...that trucker. That was the one that really got to me.

Of course, Ernie Martin was a little bastard who couldn't take a hint when he got one. Of course, he put other people's lives in danger. But, he never actually killed anyone, or even caused any kind of accident as far as I could ascertain. I'd looked up his record: two speeding tickets and a fine for using his mobile while driving. There were thousands of others like him. Killing him was a step too far. Way too far.

I drove home and went to bed but didn't sleep much.

At work the next morning, I texted Garry and asked him to meet me in the car park. Ten minutes later I stood facing him, my stomach churning. He could be a feisty fucker and really knew how to handle himself in a scrap. I'd seen him first hand when his dander was up; a fearsome sight to behold. I needed to find out without sparking a dangerous reaction.

"How's it going, Garry?"

"Fine, mate. How's you?"

"Yeah, ok."

An awkward silence ensued. It might only have lasted a few seconds but it felt like I had time to recite the entire works of Shakespeare before Garry prompted me.

"So, what's up, Steve? Why did you ask me to meet you?"

"It's a bit delicate, mate. I don't want you to overreact but I need to ask you something, ok?"

He frowned. "What are you going on about, Steve? Just ask me whatever it is you want to know. If I can help, I will."

"Are you Citizen V?"

He frowned again, then grinned, then burst out laughing.

"Hahaha! For fuck's sake, mate, that's absolutely priceless! Citizen V? Hahaha! What a belter! No you wanker, I'm not Citizen V. Why the fuck would you think something like that?"

He continued to laugh and shake his head. A very genuine reaction. I was good at reading liars; the job gave you that skill in shovelfuls.

"It's just, well, you're the only one who knows about all of my exploits. Whoever is doing this is watching what I do and then upping the ante punishment-wise. You're always slagging me off for being a pussy. I put two and two together..."

"...and got six you daft sod! You *are* a pussy but I would never go as far as killing someone. I'm a copper for fuck's sake! It would look pretty bad on the CV don't you think?"

I also started laughing and we indulged in a manly hug.

"I'm sorry, mate. I've been spooked by this whole thing. I want answers. I need to know who the fuck is behind this stuff."

Garry abruptly became thoughtful and quiet. He looked at the floor with hands on his hips, gently tapping his toes.

"What is it?" I asked him.

"It *might* be her..." He avoided my gaze again as my thoughts went into overdrive.

It might be. Again, I worried about my lack of intuition. Surgically precise. She knew about my exploits through pillow talk and she always reacted enthusiastically. Maybe a little too enthusiastically?

Abby was a wild bitch. Having a posh education, a good job and a plummy accent provided no hindrance as far as outrageous sexual behaviour was concerned. She could be impulsive too, daring me to do things I'd never normally think about, never mind do. The headphones thing actually came from her...

All that might be true but could it really be her? A massive wave of insecurity and doubt crashed over me, like a rookie surfer caught in a rip tide. Maybe Garry *was* a liar? What if this was another of his tricks? Now I'd worked out what he was up to he first denied it, then tried to deflect the blame onto Abby.

"Aw, come on, Garry! Really? I know you don't approve of Abby, and you think I'm a dick for playing away from home, but why would she?"

He looked up at me.

"Because she's a fucking psycho, that's why!"

I was taken aback by this outburst. His antithesis clearly much greater than I thought it might be.

"Look, mate, I said this was a bit delicate and it's certainly turned out that way. Let's just cool off. I'm sorry I asked you. It's clearly not you but I can't believe it's Abby either. I'll see you later when we go out on patrol, ok?"

He looked at me and shrugged. As he walked away towards the station building I heard him mutter, "Pussy!"

I let it ride, heading back into the building a few paces behind. I needed time to think. Rather than resolve anything, the last few minutes seemed to have made things worse.

I spent all day fretting over the situation with Garry. Communication between me and my partner got pretty monosyllabic. We did our job but not much more.

The seed he planted regarding Abby germinated, then grew hour by hour, developing in my mind like a triffid. I was due to meet Abby that evening and, for most of the day, I had no idea how I was going deal with her. I imagined confronting her with accusations of being Citizen V would be a damn sight harder than it was with Garry. I just couldn't get my head around the idea. I didn't want to get my head around the idea.

In the circumstances, I decided it would make sense to simplify my life and dump Abby. My head pulsed with enough complications and potential unexploded bombs. I didn't need the stress of worrying when she might light the fuse to her pile of ordinance. Anyway, it was only ever a sexual thing. I had no deep feelings for her and made no promises. I wasn't prepared to abandon my wife for something as trivial as getting my end away more exotically than normal - no matter how enjoyable. If Abby did turn out to be Citizen V, I would need to find some way to deal with it.

I rang the doorbell of Abby's flat and waited. A buzz and click signified the door opening and I made my way up to her floor.

Abby stood in the doorway, dressed in nothing but the skimpiest of nightdresses. She greeted me with a deep, passionate kiss, shoving her hand down my trousers. In any other circumstances, this would have been all the encouragement I needed to indulge in hours of wild and frenzied lovemaking. However, for once, my mind was not on my groin, or hers for that matter.

I pulled away and walked towards the living room.

"Stevie, baby, what's the matter?" she cooed.

"Come through, I need to talk to you," I replied.

She followed, appearing rather crestfallen.

"That sounds a bit...ominous..." she said rather softly.

Without replying I walked across the living room and helped myself to a scotch from the crystal decanter, which always sat on the solid oak coffee table.

"Do you want one?"

She nodded and I poured a second large measure of the amber liquid, popping a dash of coke in it. Sacrilege, as far as I was concerned, but how she liked to drink it.

Abby took the glass and tried again to kiss me but I moved away and sat on one of the very fancy leather recliners.

"Sit down, Abby. There's something I need to say to you."

Her eyes were dampening and I could see her trembling.

"This is very hard to say, but I need to stop seeing you."

Her lip wobbled and a tear spilled down her cheek.

"I'm really sorry, it's been fun but I have issues in my life that I need to sort out and our affair is a complication I can't deal with."

"Stevie, baby, what are you saying? I love you and you love me. Whatever it is, I can help you. Let me help you, baby!"

She stood and tried to sit in my lap but I pushed her away.

"No, Abby, it's no use. It's nothing you've done," I lied, "and it's nothing you could help me with. It's been great, but I need to sort my life out. You'll be fine without me."

Her face darkened and she stood back a pace.

"You absolute bastard! You've used me. After all I've done for you! I bet that bitch of a wife is behind this isn't she?"

I stood up and started for the door.

"Abby, I know you're angry, so I'll ignore that. I have to go now. Please take care and try not to be too bitter about this. I never promised you anything. It was fun but we never had a future, I thought you knew that?"

She sobbed violently, "Stevie, please, I'm sorry. Please don't go! I love you. We can make this work. If you need some time, I can wait."

As she tried again to wrap herself around me I opened the door.

"No, Abby, I'm sorry it's over. Goodbye. I hope you

find someone that makes you happy."

I didn't want to wait for the lift, so I made for the stairwell.

"You will be fucking sorry! You bastard! I'll make you very fucking sorry!" Abby screamed.

I ignored her, took the steps two at a time, eventually crashing out into the street, my heartbeat setting a tattoo for my thoughts. I'd managed to bottle out of asking her whether she was Citizen V but I found it hard to care. I needed to get out of there, sort myself out.

Abby Hester sat down heavily on her couch, blew her nose, wiped her eyes. She slurped a mouthful of scotch and coke. She didn't even like scotch. It was only in the flat for his sake. Jesus, why did he think she drowned it with coke? How much more of a hint did he need, the selfish prick. It turned out all her cynical, singleton friends were right - men were indeed all bastards. However, this particular bastard was going to regret making her feel like this.

She got up and went through to the bedroom, changed out of her negligée and put on clothes more suitable to going out in public. Repairing her smudged make up, Abby looked in the mirror and steeled herself. She was better than this, sobbing over a bloke. A married, lying bastard of a bloke at that. She had things to do, things to finish off. He might think he could just walk away and leave her but he was wrong. Very wrong.

**

Bubba managed to convince Leo to calm down a bit on the drive across town. It was pointless wading into this situation without proper planning and forethought. Bubba used a long-cultivated contact inside the Met to get some gen on the cop in the video. Turned out the cop in question worked in the Armed Response team and could potentially be a dangerous adversary. Not only that, but he comprehensively decked Leo in their last encounter, and was bound to be handy in a scrap. One thing Bubba learnt in the years spent minding clubs and pubs - never underestimate your opponent. If you did, you'd very likely end up in A&E or under the ground. They arrived outside the police station and waited to see if their quarry would emerge.

Sure enough, before too long, the guy in question appeared and got into his car. He drove off and Bubba followed.

"Don't fucking lose him, Bubba! This wanker's going to get what's coming to him."

They followed him across town - ending up in Knightsbridge where he parked in front of a very fancy and expensive looking apartment building. This was interesting and surprising. No cop could afford to live in such a place and, according to the information Bubba obtained surreptitiously, the guy was supposed to live out in Surrey somewhere. Leo could smell leverage and it made him smile.

Bubba stepped from the car and walked as briskly as he dared, trying hard to avoid attracting the cop's attention. He only managed to see which row the buzzer the cop pressed was on, rather than the actual one. Once he went inside, Bubba walked up and looked at the names on the door. There were two flats on the top floor. One belonged to a Colonel & Mrs Bartholomew, the other to a Ms A. Hester. Bubba was certain he knew who the cop was visiting. He walked back to the car and reported his findings to Leo.

The cop only spent about fifteen minutes inside. A lot less than they'd expected after Bubba remarked, and Leo agreed, that he was likely shagging some posh bird in there. Maybe he suffered problems with premature ejaculation? This made Leo smile too. He could combine that with a premature death.

"Bubba, let's just wait a minute and see what happens. You've got his address and we know what station he's working from. I have an idea that will make my revenge even sweeter."

"Ok, Leo, you're the boss."

"Yes, I am, Bubba. Yes, I am."

24. DISCOVERY

When the phone rang, I was sitting in the front room, sipping a beer and watching a re-run of The Walking Dead Season 1. The number displayed perplexed me. First of all, it was eleven o'clock in the evening. Secondly, the number was not a stored contact or one I recognised. Normally, I would have cancelled the call or let it go through to voicemail. But, I was on edge...suspicious. Something made me think I should take this call.

"Stevie?" Abby sounded very strange.

"Abby? What the hell's wrong?" I hissed, instinctively lowering my voice. My wife was asleep in bed but I couldn't take unnecessary chances.

"Stevie! Please help me..."

The line went dead. I looked at the screen, dumbfounded. What the hell just happened? I knew Abby was upset when I left but this was something else. It didn't sound like heartbreak; it sounded like terror. Adrenaline flooded into my system, my stomach flipped over, my skin flushed, my heart raced and I felt a prickle of sweat forming on my nape and top lip.

Should I call back? I froze. Then the phone rang again.

"Hello?"

"Stevie?"

This time it was a man's voice.

"Yes, and who's this? What's wrong with Abby?"

"Abby's fine and she'll stay that way as long as you do

what I tell you. Do you understand?"

Caught totally off-guard, my brain struggled to make sense of what was happening. Was this some surreal dream or parallel universe I'd been pitched into?

"Well, do you understand?"

It was at times like these that all those hours of training to keep calm and manage your emotions came into force. I gathered myself, tried to wrest back some control.

"Yes, ok. What the fuck is this all about?"

"Listen to me, you piece of shit! You're in no position to be getting shirty or smart-mouthed. I have your posh tart here and, if you don't do exactly what I say, the only thing she'll be spreading for you is her blood, all over the floor."

He was riled and I needed to play it canny.

"Ok, ok. Don't hurt her. She's not done anything wrong. What do you want from me?"

"Oh, Stevie, Stevie, Stevie. What do I want? I want you to think back to that night in Cardoza's."

My mind replayed the whole evening at hyper-speed. Fuck! This was the guy I'd given a mobile phone enema to.

"The night you thought it would be a good idea to teach me a lesson you sonofabitch!"

The voice overflowed with malice and I recognised it from the restaurant. I still couldn't place the guy though. Leon or something his voicemail message said.

"Well, guess what? I'm going to return the favour. I'm going to teach you a very valuable lesson about fucking with Leo Corantelli!"

I nearly dropped the phone. Oh, my, fucking, god! I had attacked the son of one of the most well-known gangsters in London. The name on the voicemail...Leo. At the time it made me uneasy and now I knew why. Stay calm, think clearly, breathe normally.

"Look, Leo, I'm sorry but you were bang out of..."

"Don't you dare start trying to justify yourself or lecture me you fucking cocksucker!" he screamed as he cut me short. "You stop talking and start listening. I want you to go and stand in the street outside your house, right now. Don't try and phone anyone, don't bring a weapon or a phone or anything else with you. Just you, in what you're wearing now, outside, right now! Got it?"

I tried to stall for time.

"I can't just leave right now, my son's in bed and my wife's out. I can't leave him alone." I lied.

"Stevie, you must think I am one stupid, dumb, fuck! Well, do you, Stevie? Do you think I'm a stupid fuck?"

"No, Leo..."

"It's Mr Corantelli to you, you fucking shithead. Get outside, now! My man will be there in one minute. If you're not outside when he gets there, I'll spend the next week posting you pieces of poor, little Abby. Ok? You got it now, Stevie?"

"Yes. Don't hurt her. I'm going now."

"See you soon, Stevie. I am *so* looking forward to seeing you again."

The line went dead.

I grabbed a piece of paper and scribbled a note on it for my wife.

Big trouble. Phone guy was Leo Corantelli! Tell Garry. S x

I placed it prominently on the kitchen worktop. I retrieved my small pen knife from one of the drawers and forced it down inside my shoe. It made walking painful and, in truth, it wasn't much of a weapon, but I had to take the chance. I quickly texted Garry.

Abby kidnapped by Leo Corantelli. He was phone in arse guy. In big trouble. Need help. Just you!

I looked at the phone. Should I risk taking it? I had to. I was going to be up against it as it was. The idea that getting caught breaking the rules on weapons and phones would make things worse, seemed unlikely. He could only kill me once. I switched it to silent, turned off the vibrate function and shoved it down the front of my shorts. Even the most enthusiastic frisk should avoid a direct hit on my genitals. Closing the door behind me as quietly as possible, I walked to the pavement outside my house and waited.

***

Stark stood in front of the evidence board, chewing on the marker pen he'd just used to amend the information on it.

"Right then, Katz, let's just look at this again."

The detective constable was sitting in a chair a few feet away. They were the only two people in the room.

"We've got four victims; all from varying social backgrounds, race and ages; all male. So far, the locations of the attacks are pretty sketchy. We know where the victims were picked up or dropped off, but not where they were taken to be mutilated. We don't have a connection between them yet do we?"

His partner shook her head.

"No, we've got no obvious connections anyway. We have notes written in the singular but two of the attacks - the one on Dwayne and the one on Ernie Martin - might have involved two offenders. Saying that, it seems like maybe Dwayne got muddled up and has offed an innocent man. How am I doing so far?"

"So far, so not good, sir. This case is becoming a nightmare. The thing is a jumble of victims and motives. We're short of so much information that could help."

Stark was thinking pretty much the same thing. They really needed some sort of eureka moment; a flash of inspiration or insight which up until now had evaded them.

"Aye, it's a right bloody mess, Katz. Let's think though. Is there something we've missed?"

They dropped into silent contemplation, reading the names, addresses, and other details of the attacks that were posted on the board. Trying to draw meaningful conclusions from what was up there.

"Sir, this Citizen V character?"

"Aye?"

"He was pretty big on publicity for his cause, right?"

"Aye."

"Well, maybe there's something online? A website or something like that?" offered Katz.

"Ok, not a bad idea - it's definitely worth a trawl. You do a bit of that and see what you can come up with.

"Oh, I know what I meant to ask you. Did we get anywhere with the CCTV footage from the Tube station where Calvin Jacobs was killed?"

Katz shook her head again, "No, sir, it was too crowded. We thought we might be able to zoom in and enhance but it's not like that American CSI bollocks on the telly. There was nothing of any use and too many people right next to the victim to possibly identify a single attacker. Three of the people closest to him were wearing hoods and their faces were totally obscured."

"Shit. Ah, well, another dead end. Right, I'm going back to talk to Dwayne. You get on with seeing if you can dig something up online."

"Yes, sir."

Katz began by putting Citizen V into the search engine and sat back as a huge list of links were thrown up. Most of them involved newspaper articles. There were forums and message boards galore; full of the usual incoherent nonsense either supporting or damning the vigilante. Most of this stuff got posted by wind-up merchants, imbeciles or drunken students in the early hours of the morning. It would take ages to trawl through that shitpile in pursuit of diamonds.

There was the predicted merchandise for sale. T-shirts with legends proclaiming, "I Am Citizen V" and another recommended for Stag nights which read, "No, I Am

Citizen V". Katz could just picture the group of lads standing in a row and spoofing the famous scene from Spartacus. There were some more confrontational designs including, "Don't Fuck With Me, I'm Citizen V", guaranteed to bring trouble to the door of any wearer.

The YouTube link caught her eye because it appeared on the first page. That meant it must be getting a lot of hits and re-posting etc. As she watched the video unfold, Katz felt a tension form in her jaw. The video featured Luke Pritchard prior to the removal of his ears. The guy who confiscated his phone, then returned it after chastising him, looked so familiar. It couldn't be...could it? She watched it three times on the trot and by the third viewing she was absolutely convinced of the guy's identity. This was not good. Seriously not good. She closed her laptop and went to find Stark. The repercussions were going to be immense as far as the reputation of the Met was concerned. The fall-out could be of Chernobyl proportions.

Katz never saw Stark's face as pale before.

"Oh, fuck!"

"Oh, fuck indeed, sir. I had a very similar reaction when I realised what I was looking at."

"Hargreaves is going to look like that girl from the Exorcist!"

"Sorry, sir?" asked a puzzled looking Katz.

"You've never seen...oh, crap, you're too young aren't you? It's a horror film where a wee lassie gets possessed and her head starts spinning round and, oh, never mind. Trust me, he's going to be very annoyed!

"I want you to try and find out - subtly for now - where Steve Welch is. Check when his next shift is and we'll make preparations to do this quietly and with as little fuss as possible. The last thing we need is the media managing to get wind of it before we're ready to deal with them."

Katz made a small salute and walked off. Stark was sure

the thaw was increasing. He had to stop thinking like this. The lass was too young for him, he was her boss and he was up to his proverbials in a very difficult case. He made his mind up to go out and get laid that very evening. Well, as long as he wasn't too busy working of course.

***

Garry Black was up late and looked at the text in disbelief. What the hell was this? Some kind of sick joke on Steve's part?

He texted a reply along those lines and waited.

Ten minutes passed and no reply came.

He phoned but it went straight to voicemail.

Garry began to feel his nerves responding. Mouth drying out, tension gripping at his muscles. He remembered the hilarious story Steve told him about the guy in the restaurant. He realised this guy must have been Leo Corantelli and now Steve, the king of sweet revenge, was about to taste someone else's sugar.

The dilemma almost overwhelmed Garry. If he really had attacked Leo Corantelli, Steve would be in grave danger. It was unprovable-in-a-court-of-law, common knowledge that Leo Corantelli was involved in the disappearance of at least two men; presumed deceased. The text asked Garry not to get anyone else involved but that would put *him* in danger of two things: death or serious injury thanks to Leo, or the end of his career. What a great choice!

He wondered what Steve would do in his position and decided the big man would try to help. There was one major stumbling block to all of this though. Garry had no idea where to look. He couldn't just access the files on Leo Corantelli; he'd need to ask for permission. As soon as he asked, he'd be interrogated as to why and he couldn't think of anything plausible other than he was working on a case. But, the response team didn't really work on cases. By it's very nature it was not proactive and did not investigate. They were there as trained, armed back-up for unarmed colleagues in difficult situations. If he asked the wrong person, they'd be onto him like a sniffer dog in a crack den and, before he knew it, he'd be standing in front of the Chief putting Steve and Abby's lives in jeopardy. Even if he did find a less inquisitive helper, prepared to waive him through computer security, what the hell would he look for? It's not as if Corantelli would be dealing with Steve at his house or a legitimate business premises.

Garry felt a feeling of impotence and frustration that almost overpowered him.

There was really no other way, he needed to get some help. He'd likely get into trouble for not reporting Steve for the assault on Corantelli but so be it. He couldn't just go off to bed and wait for the inevitable phone call in the morning informing him of the death of his friend. Slipping on his jacket he left his wife asleep upstairs and got into his car. It wasn't a murder case...yet...but he decided he needed MIT's help anyway.

***

I was in the car now; my hands tied and a bag over my head. One of them put a gun to my temple, making sure I laid down low on the back seat. This was not good.

It's amazing how many different types of thought go careening through your brain in such situations. Work, home, family, all manner of crazy schemes to make your escape, death. Yet, so few of them are helpful; in a practical or emotional sense.

I couldn't tell where we were going thanks to the combination of sensory deprivation and stress. It proved too difficult to judge how much time had elapsed before the car came to a halt. I thought perhaps an hour and a half but it could have been a lot more or a lot less.

There was a sudden, intense pain in my skull and

everything went black.

25. COME ON AND RESCUE ME

The bar thrummed to the soundtrack of a DJ in one corner. A young guy learning his trade, one hand holding a headphone earpiece in place, the other fiddling with his decks. The music was not really to Stark's taste but stomaching it was a means to an end.

Stark sat at the bar, sipping on his diet coke. Giving up alcohol had been difficult. Not many people took his abstinence seriously at first - a Scottish teetotaller? Aye right! His pals ripped the piss out of him more relentlessly than usual for a time but, eventually, Sheena became their slagging of choice.

Being sober helped him do a better job but it allowed him to overwork. He could never cry off a job on the basis that he was incapable of driving or making lucid decisions. But, the real reason he abstained was Carrie. His beautiful twin sister. His best friend. His crushing guilt.

Carrie's boyfriend, Frank Massey, ran his own insurance brokerage. Separated, father of three teenage kids and ten years older than her. No-one approved of their relationship, with his mother being particularly vehement in her objection. Stark always felt uneasy in the guy's company; boastful, overbearing and one of those people who'd always try and outdo you if you relayed an amusing anecdote or slightly tall tale. He liked a drink.

No-one realised what was going on until it was too late. It started as psychological abuse. Controlling, jealous, unreasonable outbursts and restrictions placed on her social life. Friends were gradually excluded and discarded. The family were next. Stark found it harder and harder to make contact with Carrie or engage her in a conversation if she did happen to answer her phone. Slowly, they became estranged. Then, it turned out, the physical abuse began in earnest. He should never have let it happen. He should have known.

He was working when her call came through, an incoherent, rambling, outpouring of regret and apologies. Stark's alarm bells rang and he flew to her. Smashing down the door of the flat, he crashed into the bedroom, where she lay motionless on top of the covers. Blue lips, translucent pallor, chest stilled. Frantic resuscitation attempts by him, then an ambulance crew, failed to rouse her. Things were never the same again.

The woman came into the bar with two friends. Small, blonde and buxom, definitely his type. The smile shone from her face like a flashlight whenever she broke it out. Stark engaged eye contact, returned the favour smile-wise and they got chatting. He still had it.

She was fun, ditzy and enthusiastic. All the signs were pointing to an end to his drought and a chance to release some of that pent-up frustration causing his lusting after Katz. Then the phone rang.

***

Garry Black stood in the station locker room donning his gear. The call to DI Stark had been a bit difficult. The poor bastard was out on the pull when Garry called and, according to him, about to go home with the best looking girl in the bar. However, as Stark didn't drink, he was able to come straight over to the station. It was not for Garry to know that on that very afternoon, Steve had become a wanted man by his own side. When he explained what

Steve did to Leo, it only confirmed to Stark that Welch was their Citizen V. At least, it would once they'd rescued him from an immensely pissed-off gangster.

Stark also made a difficult call - to the DCI. Hargreaves' permission to go after Welch was vital and, despite the lateness of the hour, it would have annoyed him a whole lot more if Stark ploughed on without it. Thankfully, the Chief's reaction was softened because he already witnessed the wayward cop's exploits on YouTube. There would be no way for Hargreaves to outdo the levels of vexation he demonstrated once he reached the end of that little horror show.

Garry expected to be sent home and be put on report for failing to inform anyone of Steve's exploits. In a time of surplus manpower and unlimited budgets, that may well have happened but, as the clock ticked past 1am, DI Stark needed every available, trained officer he could get his hands on. The reprieve was only temporary mind you, Garry knew that, but the priority now lay with finding Steve and Abby before Leo Corantelli got carried away. He didn't care much for Abby Hester but he didn't wish her any real harm.

Stark, Katz and a couple of other cops gathered in the briefing room. Stark laid out the basic situation regarding the alleged kidnap of a fellow officer. Right now, he was waiting on a call from the Serious Organised Crime Unit or SCD7 as it was shortened to internally. They were currently working on a long-running case against the Corantelli family and their associates. The chief of the unit spoke to Hargreaves and agreed his team would cooperate in the rescue of Steve.

Stark addressed the slowly increasing bevvy of cops.

"Ok, here's where we're at. We have a police officer and his alleged mistress, kidnapped by a very grumpy gangster. This is not a good combination of factors.

"Unluckily for him, and luckily for us, the SCD7 have

been tailing Leo Corantelli recently and have a fix on his vehicle. The car has been located in Essex at a farmhouse on the outskirts of Chelmsford. We need to get organised and get out there as quickly as we can. We think from the text message, sent to Sergeant Black, that our target already has about an hour's head start on us and that's only going to grow. Every second lost might be critical."

Stark paused, little noise coming from the audience; a picture of intense concentration.

"Right, you all know the drill. The Armed Response Team will lead the way. Good luck and stay safe."

There was a rousing chorus of 'yes, sir!' and various other exclamations of agreement before the room cleared and everyone made for their vehicles.

In the car, Katz and Stark hardly exchanged a word. The darkness was riven by the snake of red and blue lights. Sirens blared intermittently as dozy, early morning drivers failed to look in their mirror, or failed to notice the approaching column and made to pull out of junctions or enter roundabouts.

In the lead vehicle, Garry checked his weapon for the umpteenth time as the metropolis of London faded behind them and the open country of rural Essex opened out either side of the road. The tension was building enormously. Garry began biting his fingernails, which drew a disapproving look from his driver for the evening. It reminded him of that guff people spouted about there being more bacteria under your fingernails than there was in a toilet. For want of a better word - shit! He'd run the risk of biting his nails any day over licking the bowl.

The radio operator guided them in via the satellite tracking system and, as they got within a half mile, they switched off the lights and sirens. Then, as they rounded a corner, the ground dropped away below them and Garry saw the farmhouse.

Lights were on in at least two downstairs rooms and

one upstairs. The building looked substantial; brick-construction, two storeys high and set back from the road in at least an acre of ground. There were three vehicles in the driveway - a black BMW, a black Range Rover and a small, light-coloured coupé which he wasn't sure about and couldn't decide between a Hyundai or a Kia.

They stopped a few hundred yards short of the house. Stark ran up to the two lead vehicles containing the armed officers.

"Right, has anyone had a look with night vision?"

The team leader, Don Pierce, got out of his car to talk to Stark.

"Yes, DI Stark, we've had a look. There are three vehicles but we haven't seen any people yet. There's been no movement across any of the windows and, as far as we can tell, the vehicles are unoccupied."

Stark looked at his watch; it was two-thirty. The kidnappers would have had more than enough time to kill Steve if they were so minded. If they'd been torturing him, then who knew what sort of state he might be in. The paramedics were on stand-by, with an ambulance parked about a quarter of a mile away in case they needed it. He was pretty sure they would.

"OK, we don't have a lot of time; an officer's life is in danger here, a civilian as well as far as we can tell. What do you think, Don?"

The AR team leader only took a second or two to respond, he'd spent the journey working through scenarios.

"I'll take my team in quietly. We'll do as quick and thorough a recce as we can, ensure the vehicles are secured, then I'll send four in the front and two in the back. Have the rest of your lot ready to follow as soon as we give the signal, ok?"

"Right, understood. Good luck, Don."

Pierce nodded, got back in his car and the AR team drove down to the front of the house.

When the team got to the entranceway, Pierce noticed the security lighting on the outside of the building. If they were to proceed any further the place would light up and they would lose any chance of taking the kidnappers by surprise. He took out a small, lightweight air pistol and shot out the bulb. It popped rather more loudly than he'd have liked and a few seconds later he realised he was holding his breath while he waited for a reaction. Nothing and no-one stirred. He exhaled.

Pierce gathered the team, indicating that four of them, including himself and Garry, would assault the front, while the other two officers would go around the back of the building. With a couple of gestures, they crept forward across the driveway towards the parked cars: all three vehicles were locked and unoccupied.

Garry made his way to the window, crouched down below it. He held up a small mirror, tried to get some sort of view inside. The curtains were fully shut and he could not make anything out. This would put them at a disadvantage. They had no schematic of the building and no guarantee the layout would be sympathetic to them storming in.

Pierce's radio suddenly erupted in his earpiece, making him start, even though the officer was whispering.

"Sir, this is McGowan. We have two hostiles down outside the back door. Over."

"Ok, McGowan. We're going in the front. Proceed with due caution on my command. Over."

The front door had no handle, which meant the lock engaged when it was pulled to. One of the team took a small battering ram and smashed it against the door as Pierce shouted, "Go! Go! Go!"

The door gave way easily and the four officers moved in with weapons raised and adrenaline surging. At the back, the other two team members also made their way inside. On the road outside, Stark and his team set off with sirens blaring and lights flashing.

"Armed police! Lay down your weapons!" shouted Pierce as they walked through the hallway.

The first room on their left was a small drawing room with bookshelves, a heavy, oak desk and a couple of leather easy chairs. No kidnappers.

In the first room on the right, they walked into a scene of utter devastation. It was a much larger lounge with a smattering of appropriate furniture.

A woman, presumably Abby Hester, sat tied to a dining chair; unconscious or dead. A burly man lay on the floor with a pool of blood framing his head. In an armchair, sat Leo Corantelli, his head lolling backwards and his throat cut from ear to ear like some kind of gruesome, exaggerated smile. In the middle of the floor stood Steve Welch, blood dripping down his hand and arm and a strange, faraway look in his eyes.

"Drop your weapon!" shouted Pierce.

Steve let the flick-knife drop to the ground and just looked at them blankly as Stark and Katz burst into the room.

"I, I...." was all he could muster before he was cuffed and taken out to a car.

Stark looked around him in shock.

"Holy crap, Batman! This is going to take a bit of explaining away don't you think?" The rhetorical nature of the question being observed by all present.

"How's the girl?"

One of the AR team looked back at him and said, "Weak pulse, but breathing and alive, sir."

"Good, get the paramedics in here now and let's clear the place for SOCO. They are going to be *very* busy boys and girls tonight!"

26. A HARD CASE

The thought of interrogating Steve Welch troubled Stark. He was one of their own, with an exemplary record - even a couple of commendations for bravery in the line of duty. What the hell was the guy thinking about with all this vigilante nonsense? Stupid and nonsensical as that was though, it wasn't the worst of it. To follow all that up with the slaughter (and there was no other word for it) of those guys at the farm...that took a certain kind of mindset. There had been talk of getting a shrink in but Stark managed to persuade the DCI to let him talk to Welch first. Katz would sit in with him for the experience, under strict instruction not to contribute.

The interview room looked no different than normal but, at the same time, nothing like normal. His chair scraped the floor as he pulled it back to sit down and the noise nearly cut Stark in half. He'd been less nervous doing his first interview all those years ago.

Welch, sitting forward in his chair, with hands clasped together on the table top, rolled his thumbs round each other incessantly and chewed on his bottom lip. His clothes were articles of evidence now and, as a result, his outfit consisted of a rather unflattering set of white overalls. He looked tired and overwrought; his eyes wet and bloodshot, his skin blotchy and dry. As Stark prepared his papers it struck him that Steve Welch was a big man - brawny. The kind of guy you'd want at your side in a

153

serious situation. The kind of guy to be careful not to cross.

Once again, he fired up the tape and completed the formalities.

"Steve, I have to tell you that this is a first for me in more ways than one."

The big firearms officer didn't engage Stark with eye contact.

"I've interviewed a couple of coppers for things before but nothing on this scale and no-one as senior as you." Stark paused but there was still no response or acknowledgement.

"I understand you've had nothing to say for yourself since we brought you in. Well, now's the time for that to change. I need you to try and explain what the hell happened in the farm house first, then maybe, once we've shed some light on that débâcle, we can move onto the Citizen V stuff?"

Welch shuffled uneasily in his seat, sat back, looked up at the ceiling and sighed.

"What is it, big man? Boring you, am I?" snapped Stark.

The other cop slowly lowered his head to look directly at Stark and smiled wearily.

"Look, DI Stark, it's quite simple, I don't remember anything about the farmhouse. One minute I was being coshed in the back of a car, the next I was standing in the middle of a room full of dead bodies and cops. I have absolutely no idea what happened in between."

Stark snorted. "Come on, Steve, you'll need to try harder than that. Jesus man, you were covered in the blood of the victims and holding a knife. It's not plausible that you have no recollection of murdering the four men in that house."

Welch shook his head, "That's all I've got. I don't know what happened. *If* I killed those guys, it was in self defence, and calling them victims is stretching the meaning of the word more than a little don't you think?"

"Whether they were fine upstanding citizens or gangland scum, it makes no difference to the law. You murdered them and you'll be going down for it."

"I don't think I did murder them!" shouted Welch, "I would need to have been compos mentis to take down four men don't you think? Four, big, well-trained men at that."

"I don't know, Steve, I'm no psychiatrist but I think it's much more likely you're lying to me and you are perfectly aware of what you did."

This time Welch slumped back into his initial pose and started twirling his thumbs around each other again.

"Ok, let's forget about them for a minute and move onto your alter ego."

The big cop looked up quizzically.

"Citizen V, Steve, Citizen V. Then again maybe it should be Citizen W? What do you think, Welchy?" taunted Stark.

"I think you're off your head, mate. I had nothing to do with all that shit."

Stark looked at Katz, who had been remarkably well behaved so far, but she remained impassive. Impressive and delicious.

"Steve, I'm going to call a halt to this nonsense for a wee while. I'd like you to go away and have a think about how you're going to continue with this interview. I'll be back in a bit."

With that, Stark closed down the interview and headed off to the incident room. Katz tailed along after him.

***

I didn't really know what the hell was going on here. I wasn't lying to Stark when I said I had no recollection of how I got from unconscious in the car to standing amongst corpses in the farmhouse. It was a total fucking mystery. If I was tooled up for the job and alert enough, I probably could have taken those dudes down and I would have; if it was the only way to stop them from killing Abby or me. But slitting Leo's throat...with his own knife...that was something else.

I couldn't think straight. Things had spiralled way out of my control now. Garry did what he thought was right but it landed me deep in the brown stuff. The Leo situation was going to make it look like a dead certainty I was Citizen V. I didn't have a plausible alibi for the farm and when I sat and tried to work out where I'd been when the escalations of my revenge pranks took place, I had nothing concrete, nothing that would seem anything other than flimsy. Nothing that could be corroborated by a credible witness.

I was in deep trouble and I knew it.

***

Stark and Katz were back in front of the evidence board again.

"This is getting crazier by the second!"

Katz shrugged and nodded in agreement.

"He must be lying. There's no way he knows nothing about all of this. According to Garry Black, he shoved a phone up Corantelli's jacksie, for which he deserves a medal by the way, and that led to Leo kidnapping his mistress, and then abducting Welch himself. I reckon Leo had revenge on his mind but, somehow, Steve managed to free himself and take out the entire crew using a knife and some fancy kung fu shit. Afterwards, he's claiming some form of amnesia?"

"No doubt some clever shrink will diagnose a form of post-traumatic stress - probably get him off with manslaughter," Katz added.

Stark continued to state what they knew. "He's also starring in that video featuring Luke Pritchard, who was also mutilated by Citizen V."

Katz's brow furrowed.

"Sir, do you think he might be Dwayne's nemesis as well? He did say the guy who attacked him was a big, white dude."

Stark ran his hand over his jaw.

"Aye, I reckon you're onto something there, Katz. Let's get a line-up organised. If Dwayne id's Welch as his attacker, then we've nailed the bastard! That will link him directly with attacks on two of the victims. Coincidences can happen but that would be taking the fucking piss!"

"I'll get right onto it, sir."

27. IDENTITY PARADE BLUES

Stark sat opposite Welch again. Both Luke Pritchard and Dwayne Clements picked him out in their respective identity parades and Stark had no more doubts that the man sitting across the table from him was Citizen V. He just had to get him to admit it.

The tension in the room throbbed like a bruised cheekbone. All those concerned knew the enormity of a serving police officer being unmasked as a vigilante murderer. DCI Hargreaves did his usual charming job of indicating how he felt about this to Stark. He watched from behind the one-way glass that made up one wall of the interview room. He wasn't the only high profile guest. The Chief Superintendent was also observing proceedings. This was Stark's big moment; he hoped Welch would crumble quickly. He didn't.

The questioning was pretty straightforward. Did Welch kill Ernie Martin? Did he mutilate Luke Pritchard? Where was he when Dwayne Clements was abducted? Did he have any witnesses to corroborate his flimsy alibi? The answers were all short and to the point whenever he deigned to give one.

There were some indisputable facts Welch could not avoid. CCTV showed him in the shopping centre on the day of the attack on Dwayne Clement's, and the victim identified him as the assailant. Private video footage showed him taking Luke Pritchard's mobile phone from him. Once again, positively identified by the victim, as well as the person who filmed him. Subsequent interviews with Pritchard revealed the boy needed to attend Accident and Emergency to have his earphones removed after they were super-glued in place. Welch was found in the middle of the room in the aftermath of the murder of Leo Corantelli and his entourage. Additionally, his telephonic, anal insertion was confirmed by Garry Black, the restaurant manager and a couple of (admiring) staff. His rather unsympathetic answer-phone message was also retrieved.

However, Welch remained adamant he had nothing to do with either of the deaths. He also denied being responsible for any mutilations subsequent to the incidents captured for posterity by cameras or seen by eye-witnesses. This puzzled and disappointed Stark. It was making him look bad in front of his superiors; interviews had gone on with Welch for two days solid, he should have folded by now. Then again, it wasn't unusual for blatantly guilty parties to flatly deny the truth. Faced with the prospect of many years behind bars, and all that might entail, it was common for the guilty to retreat into denial - some of them actually seemed to convince themselves of their own innocence, despite their intimate knowledge of the facts. Additionally, Welch was a highly trained officer, well acquainted with any technique Stark might employ to get him to open up. However, something nagged at Stark as he made his way to Hargreaves' office.

The office was a neat freak's delight. Nothing out of place, nothing untidy. No pens out of containers, no scattered papers, no office detritus of any form really. A coaster with a picture of a cupcake on it sat waiting for a coffee mug to adorn it. The room always put Stark on edge - much like it's uniformed denizen.

Some people can only really do pissed-off well. All their other attempts at interaction fall flat or seem forced, hollow even. Hargreaves was the consummate, irritated curmudgeon.

"Right, Stark, let's stop farting about here and get a confession out of this poor excuse for a policeman!"

"I know, sir, it's very frustrating but I am a little unsure of this now..."

He never got the chance to complete the sentence before Hargreaves tore into him.

"Unsure? Unsure?" he hissed. "I didn't give you this bloody case for you to turn round and tell me you're unsure. What the hell is there to be unsure about? The lying toad is as guilty as any person I've ever seen in an interview room."

Stark decided to respond firmly but politely. It was pointless to deliberately antagonise someone like Hargreaves and Stark wanted to maintain his own dignity. The man's default was unreasonable and it would make little difference to how the senior officer regarded him, no matter how reasonable Stark's point may be.

"With respect, sir, what I meant was, I don't know for certain that he committed the follow-up crimes. He seems so plausible and convincing. It just doesn't sit right."

Hargreaves' face was a rather unattractive shade of light purple. He didn't appreciate being contradicted or interrupted and needed a resolution. For all his relish in dishing out contempt and derision, he found it very hard to cope with it when he was on the receiving end, and the Chief Super had given him a very big plateful that morning.

"Stark, I was convinced by your boss in Glasgow to take you on here, despite my misgivings that you weren't really up to it. It has become abundantly clear to me that I should have listened to myself instead of that Mancunian idiot, Smith! Get on with it! You've got one more day and then my patience finally runs out."

Stark had to control his emotions. Bryan Smith had been his mentor - his hero. Sure, after Stark's promotion and move to the MIT things went downhill for Whistler;

his maverick approach doing him few favours in career terms. But, Smith remained a giant in more ways than just his stature. Stark attended his funeral and held a cord as the coffin was lowered into the ground. It would have given him nothing but the most intense pleasure to smash the teeth from Hargreaves' mouth but it would also be just what the arrogant, bitter, little man wanted. He chose seething quietly instead and left the room.

Katz approached Stark looking animated.

"Sir, we need to get down to the coroner's office. There's been a development."

"What development?" he replied morosely. He was finding it hard to be enthusiastic about life in London in general, never mind this bloody case.

"They say they've found some DNA evidence linking Steve Welch to the murder of Calvin Jacobs."

His mood brightened slightly. This may well be the thing they needed to finally back Steve Welch into a corner he would not squirm out of.

The car screeched to a halt outside the Coroner's office but they decanted calmly. Stark was always a little anxious when Katz drove but, at the same time, it was a nice way to get the adrenaline flowing.

Professor Logan Irwin was a tall, spindly creature with wispy hair and features. He looked cadaverous - rather appropriate given his profession. Stark imagined a strong breeze might lift the old codger off his feet. However, he was also one of the country's most respected men in his field. He greeted the two cops warmly and offered coffee, which they declined.

"Sorry, Professor Irwin, but can we just cut to the chase? What can you tell us about the DNA evidence you've found?" asked Stark.

The voice matched the body. It wafted out of him in a light, husky drawl.

"Well, Detectives, we found a single hair during the original post mortem. It took a bit of finding I can tell you but find it we did. We sent it off for analysis and just this morning we received notification that it matched the profile of someone you have in custody - Steve Welch."

The Coroner pushed a graphic across the desk for them to look at.

"Statistically, it's too good a match for there to be any doubt."

Stark looked at the coloured lines on the page and the screeds of text and remembered his last visit to this building.

"Was it, er," his brain was desperately trying to dredge the pixie's name from his memory banks, "Doctor, er, Watson, at least I think that's her name, that found this evidence?"

The gaunt Coroner looked at him enigmatically.

"If you mean Dr Watkins, then yes, but, of course, we've had to remove her from the case now."

Stark looked at Katz but the bemusement on her face was like a female reflection of his own.

"Sorry?"

"Didn't you know, Detective Inspector? I thought that's why you wanted to come in to see me. She's married to your main suspect, and the owner of this hair - Steve Welch."

Stark felt his stomach fall and touch his toes, then catapult upwards over his head, before settling back in his midriff. This was the coup de grace of a case that had already hit new heights of weirdness.

"Ok, no, I didn't know that, Professor. Can I ask you where she is?"

The old man leaned back in his chair and interlocked his fingers in front of his stomach. "She's on compassionate leave. It was clearly inappropriate to have her work on the case any further and, for obvious reasons, she was very upset at discovering the evidence that might condemn her husband to prison for committing some pretty heinous crimes."

Stark and Katz were looking at each other with the kind of intensity that was normally experienced by those deeply in love...or filled with antipathy. They couldn't voice any of their thoughts in front of the Coroner but Stark was fairly certain they were thinking the same thing. Even at this moment, he couldn't help feeling aroused. He broke their gaze and returned to the conversation.

"When did she last come into work?"

"Let me see...she was here this morning...the result came in about nine...I think I decided to send her home about ten o'clock."

"Thanks, Professor. Appreciate the information and your time. We'll see ourselves out."

They shook hands and Stark and Katz left.

They took a moment to compose their thoughts but Katz spoke first.

"Sir, she might be involved."

Stark ran his hand through his hair.

"I'm not sure. She could be. There *was* something slightly odd about her but..." he tailed off.

"OK, but surely we need to at least get her in for questioning?"

He snapped out of his contemplation.

"Yes, we do. Definitely. She might have been blissfully unaware of what Welch was up to but, then again, maybe she's in it up to her neck as an accomplice.

"Welch and, therefore, Watkins live out in Surrey somewhere don't they?"

"Yes, I think so, sir."

"Right, get onto the station and organise someone from the local plod to go out there and pick her up. I'll let DCI Hargreaves know the good news while you drive our butts down to Surrey in a hurry." He grinned and she scowled.

Katz made her call and hung up as they climbed back into the car. He braced himself for the white knuckle-ride to follow...and the drive to Surrey.

28. NON, JE NE REGRETTE RIEN

Am I sorry?

No, I'm not sorry.

I would do it all again.

I believed in our campaign. We were righting the wrongs that make all our lives so intolerable. He didn't have the stomach for the harsh lessons but I could live with that. I had more than enough guts for both of us. He never knew and that would keep us both safe. It was a beautiful thing - a symbiosis of justice. Then he became one of them. A betrayer, morally bankrupt, selfish...unrepentant.

He thought he was clever. He thought I was blind, stupid or deluded. I was, and still am, none of those things. I knew about her and I had my eye and my ear on him. He was the cat in the ass hat and I needed to put him in his place.

The gangster deserved to die and my loving husband deserved to take the blame for his death. It was the ultimate revenge and an elegant solution.

It was easy enough to follow him. I was monitoring his movements through his phone and he had no idea. I tracked him to the farmhouse and well... the rest is history. As are the gangster and his gang. An unexpected bonus in terms of ridding society of parasites and despoilers.

I thought about killing her. I nearly sullied myself with her whore blood. But it was revenge enough to see her terrified, drugged and, best of all, aware that when it's all over, he'll be gone and she'll be alone. I think that lesson will be enough to deter her from any future affairs with married men.

I knew this day would come. The day I would be discovered, unmasked. I'm ready. I have prepared well. I will not go quietly into the arms of my captors. I will not acquiesce to fate. I will not be like Bub, wandering a prison yard only as far as the chains of incarceration will allow me to go. I have already fitted my length of elastic.

29. LOOSE ENDS

The M25 strangles London in a concrete and tarmac noose, choking the city to death with lane upon lane of traffic. Traffic that spends most of its time as a stuttering, solid, clod of metal, more like a modern art sculpture than a highway. Stark and Katz were only minutes into the torturous process of circumnavigating it, when the call came through to tell them Sadie Watkins was not home. Her car still sat in the driveway and her next door neighbour claimed not to have seen her since the previous evening.

"Damn! I think we can safely assume she was involved in some way. Innocent people don't go on the run," stated Stark.

"I agree, sir. I thought she was part of it as soon as the connection came up. She would have the skill to cut and sew-up our victims, she'd have access to drugs and she knows all about forensics, which would allow her to avoid leaving clues."

Something else began to nag at Stark.

"That's all true, Katz, but why would she not try and lose the hair? How could she know it wasn't hers and take the chance on getting it analysed?"

Katz frowned as she thought about it and they fell into silence and just kept driving.

"She *knew* it was her husband's," said Katz suddenly and matter-of-factly.

"She set him up?" asked Stark.

"Yes."

"Why?"

"I reckon she found out about the affair. My guess is, they were in it together, working as a team. He cheated, she found out, and then she set him up for the fall!" rattled Katz with uncharacteristic enthusiasm.

Stark told Katz to stay on the motorway for a while. Watching the embankments and slip roads that lined the M25 slide past unused, he tried to make sense of what was going on; weighing up this theory of Katz's.

"I'm just finding it hard to get my head around the scale of her activities. Are we saying she was jointly responsible for all the mutilations and deaths? It still puzzles me that Welch is so adamant he had nothing to do with the more severe stuff."

Again they fell silent, contemplating. Katz impressed Stark with the way she picked apart the case and tried to come up with plausible solutions to this most devious of puzzles. Nothing she'd put forward so far had been outlandish, naive or illogical. The feelings of attraction were swelling again. He re-tuned his mind to the task in hand.

The pixie he met a few weeks previously certainly appeared physically fit, perhaps even trained in some form of martial art, but could she really have been so ruthless...capable? He felt another thought push its way right to the front of his mental queue.

"Katz, we need to set an APB up for her and alert customs to check the airports and ferries. We might be too late of course, but we need to at least give it a go."

He pulled out his phone and made the requisite calls. Once finished, he asked Katz to stop at the next service station. Nature called and he needed a cup of tea. He also wanted to compile a list and try to ensure they hadn't missed anything vital.

***

Thanks to the stray hair, they had enough to charge Welch with the murder of Calvin Jacobs; this gave them plenty of extra time to interview him in regard to the other offences.

"Steve, where's Sadie?" asked Stark bluntly.

The big cop looked at him askance, "What?"

"It's a simple enough question, big fellah. Where's your missus?"

Welch shook his head, "No idea. At home, at work, at the shops - take your pick. She's not been in touch since I got arrested."

"Really? Why's that then d'you think?"

Welch looked at the table and shrugged.

"Is it because she knew about your affair with Abby Hester?"

Another shrug.

"Is that why she broke your little pact and set you up for the Jacobs murder?"

Welch's head snapped up, his eyes wide with genuine confusion. His mouth dropped open a little and he moved his jaw ever so slightly as if trying to form words, but failing. If this was acting then Stark was impressed.

"Oh, come on, Steve. We know you and the wife were in it together. I reckon she found out about Abby and dropped you right in the dung. She's left you to carry the can for everything and done a runner, hasn't she? She's not at home and she's not at work. I'm going to stick my neck out on this and say she's not out shopping either. Where else might she be, Steve?"

The colour drained from Welch's face, he shook his head and looked around erratically. Stark was absolutely convinced this was news to the guy. Even RADA couldn't have prepared him to give this performance.

"So, am I right then, Steve?" Stark pushed.

"I, I, don't...I've got nothing to say to you. Just get on and charge me with whatever you've got and let's get this over with," replied Welch angrily, his voice cracking slightly.

"Are you telling me you didn't know anything about Sadie's involvement in these crimes?" insisted Stark.

The big cop folded his substantial arms and glared back defiantly. Stark suspended the interview and left him to sweat for a while.

***

I don't know what to do now. Part of me thinks, of course, it was her all along. But another part of me won't embrace complete acceptance. If it *was* her, I'm both impressed and disgusted. Sure, Sadie's a tough cookie. Sure, she seemed enamoured by my pranks, but pulling all these things off would be quite something. *Why* she did such extreme things, that's what's bugging me most of all. I've rarely encountered a moral compass stronger, but the farmhouse...

Flashes of recollection flicker through my mind. Lying in the back of the car, the pain, a strange smell, the cops bursting in. Garry. The blood. Leo's throat. Nothing forms into coherence. Could she have been there? Could she have done all those terrible things? Yes, she knows a lot of fancy Ninja shit - even I would think twice about taking her on in a fist fight, but still...

The doubts gnaw at me. Maybe I did do it. Maybe I've induced some form of amnesia to avoid the truth. Maybe I'm going completely mad.

The more I think back, the more Sadie's involvement becomes plausible; well, at least in some aspects. There are anomalies, a lack of proper recollection on my part, but it *is* possible. I never even considered her when my suspicions about Garry and Abby surfaced. Sadie was not even on my radar. Apparently, she should have been.

The real kick in the studs is her disappearing act. The affair would have hurt her; infuriated her even. Was that enough? Was that what it took to make her turn on me, to try and set me up? Then again, maybe I did leave a hair on Jacobs' person after our altercation. Maybe it was just a provocation from Stark - attempting to get me to fill in his numerous blanks. I need to be on my game as far as the interview mind games are concerned. Yes, emotional manipulations on Stark's part are much more likely.

My head is swirling. So many possibilities, alternative versions of the same truth. Unreasonable doubt. It's hard to concentrate, to find a way to deal with this.

What might I gain by passing the buck? Nothing appeals to me. They need to catch her themselves, then get her to confess. I'll go down for the small stuff, that's a given. Too much evidence and too many witnesses. But, I'm confident nearly all the big stuff can be dodged. Even the Jacobs thing will be ok...it's just the farm. Thing is though, how do I prove she was there when I don't really know if she was? She's a forensics expert: I'm pretty sure she'd have left nothing to work with. Not only that, but a single fibre, a hair or any other titchy thing like that; she could argue that I carried it in after close contact with her.

If it *was* her, then by fuck, she's been clever! I cheated on her, did some stupid, reckless things, and got caught; by her and my colleagues. I need to take my punishment, suck it up and leave her to it. I won't incriminate her or use her to try and get away with it. Stark will need to sort all that out for himself - if he can. I can prove enough reasonable doubt on the murders. I'll do some time but I'll manage.

The more I've turned things over in my mind, the more I realise the cheating was the worst of all the things I did. Our love was special; I should have been content. But, like so many idiots before me, a dick took control of my senses and I let him. I deserve to lose her.

If she did those things, she deserves punishment. As much as she might try to justify it, what she inflicted on Dwayne Clements and Luke Pritchard was over the top. They were just stupid, misguided kids and what I did to them was more than enough of a warning shot. If she killed Martin and Jacobs it was way, way too much - they were arseholes but they didn't deserve to be killed for it. Leo and his gang were scum and without her intervention, me and Abby would be dead. I don't weep for them but it unsettles me to think of her being so cold, so callous. I can't be part of her capture or punishment but if it comes, then so be it.

After my betrayal, the least I owe her is my silence.

***

Stark spent another few days trying to break Welch but got nothing better than admissions to most of the petty stuff and denials of all the serious stuff; including denials of any knowledge of his wife's potential involvement. It was frustrating. Hargreaves pouted. However, plenty of actual and circumstantial evidence allowed them to try him for all the murders and mutilations - apart from Ernie Martin. No evidence emerged linking Welch to the trucker, despite Stark's certainty that he had some involvement in his fate. Meanwhile, the ports and airports came up blank - Sadie Watkins vanished.

The trial was a long and protracted affair. A complex case, with multiple witnesses and a plethora of forensics to sift through. Welch's lawyers were valiant and resourceful, arguing many of the serious charges away. Reasonable doubt came into play on more than one occasion. After eight weeks, the jury returned guilty verdicts for the assaults on Dwayne Clements and Luke Pritchard but not guilty verdicts on the mutilations. He was found not guilty of murdering Calvin Jacobs on the grounds his wife may have inadvertently contaminated the evidence with one of his hairs. However, as good as his lawyers were, they could not explain away the mass of forensic evidence suggesting he killed Leo Corantelli and his retinue. Welch claimed self defence, diminished responsibility, provocation and a number of other mitigating circumstances but, in the end, received four life sentences.

The media were predictably hyperbolic in their response. The morality and standard of modern policemen was called into question, crises invoked, and much hand-wringing and navel gazing indulged in. A couple of senior Met officers took early retirement. Promises were made to review procedures and tighten up on recruitment policy blah, blah, blah. Paranoia gripped the force for a time as colleagues began to look at each other with undue suspicion, but it soon subsided. There were more pressing matters to attend to.

Stark had seen it all before. It was hogwash. Steve Welch was nothing more than a bad egg; they cropped up in all walks of life and no amount of screening, psychological profiling or hysterical press reaction would change that. Perspective would have been a better thing to concentrate on. One officer gone bad among thousands of honest, decent ones did not a corrupt system make.

Stark felt a sense of pride in a job well done and, simultaneously, a sense of disappointment in a job half done. Lots of loose ends relating to the case were left hanging. They could find nothing of any note to link Sadie Watkins to the killing of Ernie Martin or any of the other crimes for that matter. In reality, Citizen V was probably still at large. Regardless of whether or not it was Watkins' alter ego, Welch remained adamant he never wrote any of the notes and never claimed to be on a moral crusade. It struck Stark that, in fact, the campaign Citizen V embarked upon was more like an amoral crusade. No matter her gripes and objections to the behaviour or attitudes of the victims, what she decided to inflict upon them was entirely unjustified.

The errant pathologist's name remained on a watch list, in the vain hope of her appearing at an airport or ferry terminal, passport in hand. But, if truth be told, it wasn't too hard for a resourceful or clever person to avoid all that and stay hidden. Sadie Watkins was both.

30. SIGNED, SEALED, DELIVERED

Abby Hester was delighted. Garry was coming over as soon as he finished for the day. His wife might not be quite so delighted but that was not Abby's problem. She promised herself not to get involved with any more married men, but she couldn't control where her heart led her.

The court case dragged on for weeks and she and Garry got talking one lunchtime. When Steve was convicted, they went for a drink to console one another and well, it just happened. Garry was a sensational lover. He helped her forget all about that twisted freak, Steve Welch; the dumping, the kidnapping, the horrible, kinky sex he used to force her to take part in. The revelations in court about what he'd been up to while he was with her were ghastly. Garry, her knight in shining, made her feel safe again - smitten.

The room was perfect. Candles, soft music, incense wafting its aroma gently through the air. The food would be delivered any time; the oven ready and waiting to keep it warm until her lover arrived. She looked perfect; sexy and alluring not slutty. She sipped her wine and hummed along to the CD.

The doorbell rang. Abby grabbed her purse to pay the delivery boy his tip, pressed the entry buzzer and opened the door. She waited for the lift to come up or someone to walk up the stairs - no lift, no footsteps. Nerves started jangling, her heart pounded, nausea rose up in her throat. She closed the door and bolted it, the kidnapping suddenly all too vivid in her mind's eye. She went over to the window and looked down into the street below. Nothing out of the ordinary but also no delivery van. Abby picked up the phone and called the restaurant.

"Good evening, The Golden Halo, how may I help you?"

"Hi, this is Abby Hester, I have an order due to be delivered soon. Can you tell me if your boy is here at the moment?"

"Oh, hello, Ms Hester, it's John here. I'll just check for you. One minute please."

There was a short interlude where she could hear the comings and goings of the busy little Chinese restaurant she had grown to love.

"Hello, Ms Hester?"

"Yes."

"No, I'm afraid Ade isn't there yet. He should be about ten or fifteen minutes. Is that ok?"

"Yes, yes, that's fine, thanks, John. Sorry to have bothered you," Abby replied nervously.

"Not at all, Ms Hester, it's never any trouble to help you. Are you ok?" The restaurant worker had picked up on her stressed tone.

"Yes, I'm ok, thanks. I'll be better once the food arrives," she forced a small laugh, "bye for now."

"Ok, have a good evening, Ms Hester."

She placed the phone back in its cradle and paced up and down the living room. A call to Garry from her mobile went through to voicemail but she decided not to leave a message. The paranoia and fear that swamped her after the abduction still gripped her at times like this. The therapist said it might take a year or so before she was free from its constant presence. She sniffed back a small sob and took another sip of wine.

When the doorbell rang again, she nearly jumped out of

her skin. This time, she used the intercom - angry with herself for being so casual about it before.

"Hello?"

"Hello, Ms Hester, this is Ade from The Golden Halo. I have your order."

"Ok, come up."

She buzzed him in and once again opened her door. She could hear the delivery lad's footsteps as he climbed the stairs to her flat. Something made her glance down. A small gift box sat on the landing outside her door with the initials AH written on it in black marker pen. She smiled and picked it up. It must have been Garry. What a romantic so and so; even if he did scare the bejeesus out of her in the process.

She put the box on the hall table, tipped Ade, then took the food to the kitchen, carefully placing it in the oven. With dinner taken care of, she ambled back to the hallway and picked up her gift.

In the living room, Abby settled into an armchair and pulled at the bow wrapped around the brightly coloured, cardboard container. The lid popped open and she dropped the box in horror, almost vomiting in the process. She screamed and screamed and screamed until hoarse. Stuck fast in the chair, unable to move.

A frantic knocking at her door brought her back into some form of sentient thought. Her neighbour, Colonel Bartholomew, was shouting through the letterbox.

"Abby, are you ok? Abby, what the hell is going on?"

She got up and ran, crashing into the old man's arms, sobbing inconsolably, as soon as the door was open wide enough. His wife hovered behind him looking equally concerned.

"My dear girl, what on earth is the matter?" asked the older woman.

She could only point backwards. Mrs Bartholomew crept forward into the living room. Her shriek compelled the Colonel to go to his wife's aid; leaving the weeping, shuddering Abby clinging to the door frame.

"Dear god!" he exclaimed.

On the floor, next to a bright, red, gift box, lay a dismembered penis and testicles.

***

Stark looked at the note for about the thirtieth time that day.

To whom it may concern,

The world is awash with those who cannot understand right from wrong. They gloat about their indiscretions, confident they will never be challenged, never have to pay a price. Well, enough is enough. I was here to let them know that there is a price to pay and I showed them I wouldn't just sit back and take it.

Abby appears to have a penchant for married men's genitals. So I have given her some as a keepsake. Garry won't be needing them any more.

I have tried to teach my lessons directly to those who require them, but they are for all of you to learn from.

This will be the last of my lessons.

Yours,

A concerned citizen taking action.

Citizen V was back.

Garry Black's life hung by a thread as he underwent emergency surgery, but the poor bastard was in for a hell of a shock if he pulled through. Stark thought this had to be the work of Sadie Watkins. Abby Hester screwed her husband, then had the poor taste to follow that up by shagging his ex-partner and best friend. It looked like this tipped the already deranged pathologist over the edge.

The enigmatic ending was intriguing. Was she really hanging up her vigilante boots? Equally interesting was her still being in the UK. Stark convinced himself she fled the country when she first went missing. Instead, Sadie melted into the crowd in London and went unnoticed ever since. Then again, it was entirely possible she'd made a break for it this time. Who knew what identity she travelled under or how much she'd changed her appearance.

Abby Hester went into deep shock and was admitted to hospital; under sedation and the watchful gaze of an armed guard. Stark had no idea if Watkins was serious about retirement but thought it best not to take any chances.

31. CLOSE TO ME

The nursing home was an imposing building. Formerly the residence of some staggeringly wealthy Victorian doctor or merchant, with the appearance of a small castle. Towers, with conical, slate-covered roofs stood at each corner. The sandstone brickwork and pointing looked weather worn but in reasonable condition. Windows punctuated the frontage with regularity and a huge, wooden door set in an impressive porch welcomed the visitor and resident alike.

Stark met the duty manager, Karen Stubbs, and she led them to a sun room at the rear of the building. As they walked, Stark noticed the walls were adorned with hundreds of portraits of loved ones and previous incarnations of the residents. Perhaps, this helped to combat isolation, or possibly helped in the war many would undoubtedly be waging with dementia. Whatever, it was a warming touch of humanity in a place that, if the media were to be believed, would usually be devoid of such qualities.

Karen introduced him to Ann Watkins. She sat in a high-backed, leather chair, tartan blanket draped over her legs. Stark recognised the eyes or rather the obvious inheritor's. A twinkle of mischief still glinted in these bright pools of intelligence. Time had robbed Ann Watkins of many physical traits but her mind had yet to be plundered.

"Well, at my age, a visit from the police cannot bring

anything other than bad news, so out with it young man. What do you want?"

Stark liked her. Strong, defiant and no longer tolerant of niceties.

"Yes, you're right enough, Mrs Watkins, this is not good news. I need to talk to you about Sadie."

The old woman's face dropped, her eyes moistened and she licked her lips, waiting for the follow-up.

"We have reason to believe she has been involved in several violent crimes and I'd like to know if you've seen her or heard from her recently?"

Ann Watkins looked out of the window of the sun room. Aptly, shafts of bright sunlight streamed through the windows, giving the room the warmth and glow the architect surely hoped for when drawing its plans. However, melancholy and regret chilled the air once Ann spoke.

"Oh, Sadie, Sadie. My poor, mixed-up, little girl. I haven't seen her for a couple of years. She always sends cards on birthdays and Christmas but otherwise, I have no contact with her."

Somehow, this surprised Stark. On his way here, he convinced himself Sadie would be sure to keep in close touch with her mother. Now, standing in this room, in front of this frail old woman, he felt slightly foolish at having been so confident. Guilt gnawed at him. It felt as if he was re-opening a wound, which Ann Watkins only recently managed to staunch the bleeding from.

"I'm sorry to hear that, Mrs Watkins..."

"Why? What possible impact on your life would my lack of contact with my daughter have?" she snapped, a dark cloud abruptly enveloping her mood.

The guilt bit deeper into his flesh.

"None, I suppose, sorry for the glib remark. This cannot be easy for you. However, I could really do with your help. Is there anything in Sadie's background we should know about or that might help us to find her?"

184

Mrs Watkins smoothed the blanket and ran her hand through her white hair.

"Well, Inspector, my daughter has had problems all her life with controlling her temper. She seems to think she was chosen to right the ills of society. When someone crosses her or her loved ones, she feels a compunction to act."

"Is she religious?"

"God, no! If you'll forgive the pun. She's not driven by any kind of religious belief. She's driven by something that lives inside her. A dark force that she cannot control. In her late teens, we tried to get a doctor involved but she refused to co-operate. Passed every test designed to assess her as schizophrenic or whatever. She is so clever. So very, very clever."

Stark could feel her pain. This was something no parent would want to find out about their child. The burden of knowing but parental loyalty preventing her informing.

"What exactly has she been up to?"

"I don't think I need to burden you with details. At the moment she's only a suspect, we haven't proved anything for sure."

The dark cloud whirled again.

"Don't dare patronise me, Inspector! I might be an old woman but I'm not one of those vegetables back there drooling in front of the TV! What has she been up to?"

Her eyes drilled through Stark with genuine anger.

"Ok, sorry, it's a couple of murders and a couple of mutilations. The victims appeared to have committed some form of societal faux pas, which she felt compelled to make an example of."

"Just a bloody minute," she fumed, "you're talking about that Citizen V character aren't you?"

He nodded.

Finally, the stress got to her and she dropped her chin to her chest, put her hands on her head and sobbed.

Stark immediately offered her a handkerchief, which

she took sullenly. The light gone from her eyes.

"I know this must be incredibly hard to take, Mrs Watkins, but is there anyone she might turn to in her hour of need? Family, friends, ex-workmates?"

"She is alone in this world, Inspector. Her father died years ago. She married that good for nothing cop but I thought *he* was Citizen V?"

"So did we, but it turns out he might not have been. Sadie has disappeared and we need to find her. Are you sure there's nothing else?"

The old woman repeated her blanket smoothing and hair ruffle.

"There is one thing. I'm pretty sure she never sold my house after I moved in here. She rented it out - at least, that's what she told me she'd done. She paid for me to come here when I fell over once too often. Give me a piece of paper and I'll write it down for you. She might be there, tending the bones of poor old Bub."

Stark looked at her with a deep frown of concern and handed over a page torn from his notebook.

"No, no, not what you think. Bub was her dog when she was a girl. We buried him in the back garden when he died. She loved that dog."

Stark thanked her and left. As he got into his car, he couldn't help but think he'd not just spoiled her day but, more likely, what time she had left. The guilt feasted hungrily.

***

Katz drew up in front of the house with her usual haste and slammed to a halt.

It was a run-down estate. Years of neglect from residents and successive councils slowly eroding its fabric and the spirit of anyone living there. A couple of young lads on BMX bikes recognised them as cops and beat a hasty retreat, shouting some sort of obscenity in the process and baring their arses as they cycled away through the warren of alleyways and tower blocks.

The garden was unkempt and the gate missing in action - probably long since deployed as fuel on bonfire night. The house walls were daubed in graffiti. The windows were blacked out but remained intact. It looked like a crack den or some other form of repository for the chemically dependent.

"Right, I've arranged for back-up but, in the meantime, are you happy to go in?" asked Stark.

"Of course, sir. There are two of us and more on the way, we'll be fine."

"Aye, can't help thinking about that farmhouse though. A couple of those guys were a lot more formidable opponents than us."

"True, sir, but she had the drop on them, the element of surprise. We're ready for anything she might chuck at us, and we have nightsticks and pepper spray."

Stark admired her guts, amongst other things.

"Ok, but let's put on the stab vests as a precaution and stay close."

"Righto, sir."

They donned their protective clothing and drew their nightsticks. There was no reason to suspect Watkins would have a firearm. She'd not used one so far; too messy, noisy and traceable. Stark also felt sure she needed the kindling of indignation to fuel her aggression. Well, he hoped that was the case. Unlike Katz, apprehension travelled through his bloodstream like an ice crystal; he actually shivered despite the mild air temperature.

The door appeared to be fortified. No lock pick or mini battering ram was going to get them through it. The windows were locked and nailed in place; scrapes and gouges in the frame indicating previous failed attempts by other interlopers to gain entry. Symbols in the corners of each pane indicated toughened glass and again, scratches and other marks on the glass suggested bricks being thwarted. No breaking, no entering. Totally understandable precautions in a place like this but not helpful to Stark and Katz. They would need to wait for back-up after all and call in some specialist help.

The glass-cutter did its work. A large panel came loose, allowing them access through the downstairs, living room window. A couple of big, burly cops were stationed in the back garden to prevent Watkins fleeing that way, but Stark was resigned to the idea that nobody was home.

The inside of the house was amazing. Every surface was brightly painted in white, sheets of clear plastic hung between the doorways and lined the floor. In one room, for all intents and purposes, Watkins had set up an operating theatre. An autoclave, rows of surgical implements and various other accessories adorned a couple of tables against one wall. Surgical robes and other protective clothing hung from a clothes rail.

Out in the back garden, a small area of ground looked well attended to in the midst of a sea of weeds and long grass. Doubtless, this was the resting place of Bub the dog.

They'd discovered her lair but the black widow herself was not in attendance. Stark had little doubt there would be no forensic evidence to work with here but it was still another piece in the jigsaw.

***

Despite the failure to locate Watkins, the case brought Stark temporary celebrity. However, he drew the line at the conceit of appearing in documentaries or on chat shows to discuss Welch and all the other prurience surrounding the case. It might well be the modern way, but he preferred to do his job and solve new crimes, rather than endlessly rake over an old one for the sake of entertainment. London provided plenty of opportunities to keep him gainfully employed.

Katz moved on. Seconded to the serious crimes department in Leeds, continuing her education and keeping on track for that early promotion. She was going to make a very good detective and Stark didn't doubt that sometime, in the not-too-distant future, their paths would cross again as equals. He was glad he hadn't done anything foolish like proposition her. Then again, this new, improved Adam Stark induced a touch of melancholy. Once upon a time, he'd have gone for it and hang the consequences. Once upon a time, he'd have been in with a genuine chance of having her proposition him. First man, new man, old man. Unhelpful thoughts which he gave short shrift to.

The weeks drifted on and soon there were other problems and stories occupying the headlines. Life has ever been thus.

32. CHECK OUT

The handwriting on the envelope was immaculate. Every loop and flourish perfectly placed and legible. Stark didn't think he'd ever seen such an aesthetically pleasing script before. He picked the envelope up from the top of his in-tray and slid his finger under the flap. It peeled away smoothly rather than ripping asunder. He carefully pulled the letter out, giving it the due deference the sender deserved after making so much effort to present it so beautifully.

The note was just as neatly scribed as the envelope.

Dear DI Stark,

I'm sure you long since realised my secret identity, my evil twin perhaps? However, for the record, and the avoidance of doubt, I was the so-called Citizen V. My ex-husband is guilty of none of the mutilations or murders. All of those lessons were delivered by me and me alone.

There is a fire in my belly that grew impossible to resist. Since I was a young child I could not abide injustice and the derision of bullies. I needed to make a stand, to say to ordinary, decent people that they didn't have to put up with the relentless infringement of their right to a peaceful and productive life.

I made my stand and I was proud. I do not weep for Ernie

Martin, Calvin Jacobs or Leo Corantelli. However, I let the fire of indignation become an inferno of rage and took personal revenge for a wrong done to me, rather than a wrong done to Society at large. I am not proud of that. It is time for me to extinguish the flame, before it burns completely out of control.

My ex-husband spoke highly of you and I liked how you handled yourself. I want you to have the satisfaction of resolving the outstanding matters in the case and give everyone closure. I feel that my lessons will hold more weight if I set the right example. By the same token, I will not allow you to cage me like an animal. I cannot bear the thought of being gawped at by the media and the intelligentsia; half of them desperate to flog me the other half desperate to 'understand' me.

Do not waste your time looking for that which cannot be found. Instead, be satisfied to have your answers and to have learned your own lessons.

Yours,

Dr. Sadie Watkins

A concerned citizen who took action

Stark sat down heavily in his chair, tossed the letter onto the desk in front of him and clasped his hands behind his head. He should have felt elation at finally confirming his and Katz's hunch about Watkins was spot on. Instead, he felt empty. The letter represented the final, unconventional act of the most unorthodox criminal he'd ever encountered. He felt sure they'd never find Sadie Watkins. The letter was not explicit but it looked like a suicide note of sorts; a final unburdening of guilt before avoiding any possibility of capture by taking her own life.

It was the beginning of the day but it felt like the end of an era. There was something unnervingly, personally profound about those last two lines. He stood, dropped the letter in an evidence bag, and headed for DCI Hargreaves office.

Stark had no idea what this would mean for Steve Welch. Once his lawyers saw this letter, an appeal would be launched. But, what he got off with, and what he still carried the can for, was in the lap of the gods of court.

As for Stark himself, it was time to face up to his own burdens and make some changes.

Thank You!

Thank you for buying this book - I really hope you enjoyed it. If you did, it would be great if you could leave a review on Amazon.

You can visit my website at *petercarroll.ravencrestbooks.com*, and while you are there, I'd be delighted if you also subscribed to my blog. That way, I can keep you up to date with future books and other writing adventures.

Look out for my other novels *Stark Choices*, *In Many Ways* and *Pandora's Pitbull* which are all available at Amazon.

All the best

Peter

THE SECOND IN THE ADAM STARK DETECTIVE SERIES

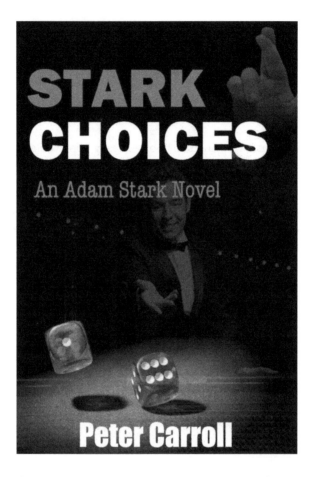

STARK
CHOICES
An Adam Stark Novel

Peter Carroll

DI Adam Stark has left London and his overbearing boss, returned to his home town of Alloa, hoping things might be quieter and to spend a bit of time with his Ma.

Meanwhile, Stella McDuff has just won millions on the lottery. It's the only good luck she's had in her entire life.

She has plans to escape to London, leaving her life of drudgery, her thoughtless children and brutish husband, Billy, behind. Stark knows the McDuffs well. Billy and his brother Malky are arch-enemies from childhood and they're not pleased to see him again.

Stella is rich, she can almost taste her freedom, but winning that amount of money has awakened a few green-eyed monsters. It's not long before she's facing every parent's worst nightmare and Stark is dealing with missing persons, kidnap, ransom and murder. So much for the quiet life back home.

Be careful what you wish for..

If you have a smart phone, scan the barcode for a link to "Stark Choices"

In Many Ways

A young man is abducted and mutilated for talking out of
turn, and a policeman is murdered as a result – all in a
day's work for Danny O'Neill, Scotland's most notorious
gangster.
Meanwhile, small-time drug dealer and shop worker Davie

Argyle has just crossed O'Neill's path. Davie has been waiting a long time for this. He needs to swallow his pride and convince O'Neill to trust him. Thing is, can he stay alive long enough for his plan to work?

Torture, murder, rock n roll and bloody revenge ensue as pasts unfurl and long-held secrets reveal themselves. In many ways, it was only a matter of time until it all kicked off...

Thriller Of The Month on www.e-thriller.com *"...following firmly in the footsteps of the pioneers of 'Tartan Noir' trail blazed by Ian Rankin and his erstwhile detective John Rebus, Peter Carroll takes us away from the prim and proper streets of the capital Edinburgh and takes us instead to the mean streets of Glasgow. Recommended and riveting reading from a relatively new author."*

If you have a smart phone, scan the barcode for a link to "In Many Ways"

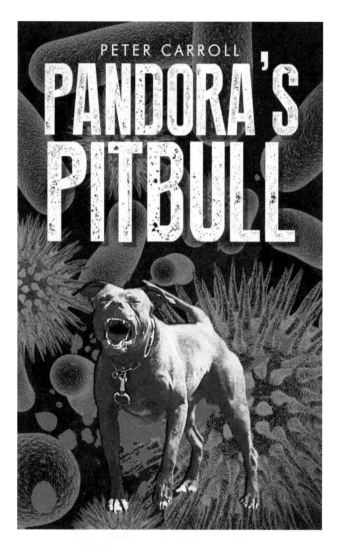

PETER CARROLL

PANDORA'S PITBULL

Two clandestine world's have collided - with disastrous consequences.

A fighting dog, kidnapped and used in a top secret experiment, is free and carrying a virus. A virus like nothing that's gone before. A virus that's spreading through Scotland unchecked.

As society implodes and people refuse to die a normal death, the fates of a small boy, a young woman, a soldier and the very country they live in will hang in the balance.

A new evil has been unleashed on the world but it might be too late to put the lid back on this particular box...
Indie Book of the Month August 2012

"Fantastic book! I absolutely love Carroll's writing style. Carroll is a true talent at writing intelligent and witty material."
RA Stephenson author of "Collapse (New America #1)"

If you have a smart phone, scan the barcode for a link to "Pandora's Pitbull"

About The Author

Peter Carroll is a Scotsman with a penchant for black humour and gritty realism. As well as writing, he's passionate about nature conservation and music.

Peter has four novels under his belt so far: crime thriller "In Many Ways", apocalyptic horror "Pandora's Pitbull", and the Adam Stark detective series, "Stark Contrasts " and "Stark Choices "

"Stark Contrasts" is his third novel.

Contact Details

Visit the authors website:
petercarroll.ravencrestbooks.com

www.twitter.com/petercarroll10

Cover designed by: Raven Crest Books

Published by: Raven Crest Books
www.ravencrestbooks.com

Follow us on Twitter:
www.twitter.com/lyons_dave